NIGHT
VISION

ELLA WEST

ALLEN&UNWIN
SYDNEY•MELBOURNE•AUCKLAND•LONDON

Allen & Unwin
83 Alexander Street
Crows Nest NSW 2065
Australia
Phone: (61 2) 8425 0100
Email: info@allenandunwin.com
Web: www.allenandunwin.com

Allen & Unwin – UK
c/o Murdoch Books, Erico House, 93–99 Upper Richmond Road
London SW15 2TG UK
Phone: (44 20) 8785 5995
Email: info@murdochbooks.co.uk
Web: www.allenandunwin.com
Murdoch Books is a wholly owned division of Allen & Unwin Pty Ltd

A Cataloguing-in-Publication entry is available
from the National Library of Australia
www.trove.nla.gov.au
A catalogue record for this book is available from the British Library

ISBN (AUS) 978 1 74331 766 2
ISBN (UK) 978 1 74336 670 7

Cover design by Astred Hicks, Design Cherry
Cover photo by Mark Owen / Trevillion Images

This book was printed in July 2015 at Griffin Press,
168 Cross Keys Road, Salisbury South, South Australia 5106, Australia.

5 7 9 10 8 6

For Trish

For Trish

This book was begun in 2010 while the author was the University of Otago College of Education Creative New Zealand Writer in Residence.

~~~~~~~~~~~~~~~~~~~~~~~~

Thanks to:

Chris Adams, University of Otago Mozart Fellow 2010 and 2011,

University of Otago Department of Music's Marama Hall Wednesday Lunchtime Concerts,

John Roxburgh, 2013 graduate of the New Zealand School of Music, Master of Musical Arts (Viola Performance)

60 Minutes documentary 'Children of the Night', reporter Liam Bartlett, producer Jonathan Harley.

THE MUSIC VIOLA PLAYS CAN BE LISTENED TO ON YOUTUBE

~~~~~~~~~~~~~~~~~~~~~~~~

One

A car has stopped on the side of the road, the noise of tyres on gravel warning me. Through the trees I see the headlights turn off. Few people travel this road, which is no more than a logging track, and none at this time of night. I let the tree trunks slide past my fingers as I go closer to see. The sun sank behind the mountains at least an hour ago, and although the twilights are stretching out as spring comes, it is dark.

The driver has got out and is looking around, up and down the road, at the forest on the other side, this side. He has dreadlocks, blond ones tied back from his face with a bandana, and is wearing jeans with holes at the knees. He needs a shave.

He is trying to see in the dark, let his eyes adjust to the starlight, the moon yet to show itself. He feels his way along the car to the boot and opens it. There is a faint glow from the light inside. He begins to yank something out, something large and heavy.

Suddenly he's startled and stops. Maybe it was the bird that flew past him? I saw it, but I know he couldn't. He pulls the something out again, this time working harder, faster, almost frantic. He gets it out of the boot and half drags, half carries it to the open driver's door and pushes it into the seat. It's a person, a man. A fat man with a beard and long hair. He's wearing a suit, a striped tie jagged around his throat. The man must be unconscious or dead. I look to see if his chest is rising and falling, or if there are any other signs of a heartbeat (like you sometimes look for in a movie when the person's supposed to be dead but is obviously not because he's really an actor so of course he's alive), but I'm too far away.

I've sat down quietly, four rows of trees in, watching, snuggled up against a trunk. That way, if he does look towards me, he will only see a strange bump against a tall pine in the dark. But he doesn't. He's too busy catching his breath. His hands are on his hips, his shoulders heaving. He's thin, maybe only half the weight of the man in the driver's seat, so he must be strong to do what he's just done. He takes other things out of the car boot, but I can't see what they are. He leaves them on the side of the road, by the trees. I am very, very still.

I know this man. Last year, in the early summer, I watched him check his dope plantation. He had carefully planted the tiny seedlings in potting mix between the tree trunks, ringed them with possum traps, probably believing that no one came into the forest.

He didn't know about me. I had come across the little garden several weeks earlier and knew enough to leave it alone. The night I saw him, he was fussing over the plants, but several weeks later everything was gone. He must have worked out that not enough light would get to the forest floor to make them ever grow well.

But now he has the car's bonnet up, doing something to the engine. He lets the bonnet fall. The noise echoes around the trees. He has forgotten to be quiet and is suddenly looking about again, wary, not that he can see anything. It's too dark. All he can do is listen. He will have to learn to use his ears and not his eyes.

Hesitating, as if he doesn't want to do it, he closes the driver's door with a soft click then reaches in through the open window and fumbles with something by the fat man. He must have turned the key in the ignition because the sound of the engine rumbles in the quiet. The headlights stay off. The man backs away and there is a loud noise and white flames. I turn away, the light hurting my eyes, and put another two rows of trees between me and the road. The glow of fire will be reflected by the night-vision goggles I'm wearing. My pale face and robotic-looking eyes will be seen.

But the man has not turned towards me. Instead, he's staring at the burning car, the brightness it has created in the night. I take the goggles off. The fire is so dazzling I don't need them. The man looks up, and so do I, suddenly our thoughts the same. Will the flames touch the trees? Will the forest burn? There is no wind and it rained last week, but not even a month of rain will stop a fire in a Canterbury pine forest.

I think the burning car is far enough away from the trees. The man must think so too because he lowers his gaze again. All of the car is engulfed now; the part where the fat man is looks as though it's burning the brightest. Is that possible? Does human flesh burn well? Human fat? I hope the fat man was dead when he was dragged out of the boot.

There is a smell, apart from the fuel and plastic and bubbling paint on metal. I don't want to think about it.

The man with the dreadlocks grabs his belongings

by the side of the forest and slips between the trees, my trees, away from the light of the fire. There's an explosion. I look back at the car. Something must have blown up. Maybe the fuel tank? It's burning fiercely now. I can feel its heat. I turn my back to it and hunt for the man, putting my night-vision goggles back on. There he is – a white intruder between the pale green of the tree trunks and the blackness beyond. Night vision turns everything into shades of green or white or grey. The goggles are heavy. At first I felt clumsy wearing them, the weight strapped to my head making me feel unbalanced. I would stumble, my neck would hurt the next day, but soon I got used to them. Now, I don't even think about it.

The goggles were my birthday present from my parents when I turned twelve. They used to be impossible to buy; the United States government controlled their legal sale to keep 'the upper hand' in night-time warfare by not letting anyone else have them. They figured out night vision when fighting in Vietnam, although it can't have been that useful because they lost that war, didn't they? I don't know how my parents got my pair, or how they could afford them. I checked on the internet – they're expensive. I spend a lot of time online. It's how I know lots of things.

The man is having trouble moving through my forest.

The light from the burning car is far behind us now, but his eyes have probably not adjusted to the darkness yet. He tries to run down a row of trees but loses his way every few minutes and bangs into trunks and branches. Once, he trips over a tree root. He should have brought a torch. He should not even be here. I wait while he gets up and brushes the pine needles off himself, and then I continue to shadow him, several rows to his left and well behind. I can see now he's carrying a spade and a bag of some sort. He keeps looking at what I think is a compass. I can see the tiny glow it gives out. We jog along like this for at least an hour. I check my watch occasionally while I wait for him to find his way again. He must have done this route before, in daylight. He seems to know where he's going.

Another logging road cuts through the forest up ahead. Will he cross it? If he does am I able to safely follow? There is probably enough light from the moon and stars to make me out on the narrow strip of gravel, if he chooses to look back.

We've come to the road and he's stopped. I linger, keeping the distance between us, worried he will hear my lungs working, my heart beating, through the whisper of the pine needles from far above. He's walking along the line of the road, just inside the trees, looking for something. There it is. Another car. With the night-vision goggles it's impossible to see what colour it is but it's large, a different make to the last one.

He's counting trees, six back from the edge of the road. I can see his lips mouthing the numbers. He drops the bag and begins to dig a hole by a tree with the spade. He works hard, frantic, forcing the blade into the stony soil between the tree roots. He takes the bandana off and wipes his face. The dreadlocks pile onto his shoulders.

He digs again, until the hole is deep and big, then he stuffs the bag in and pushes the soil back on top using his feet. On his hands and knees he scatters pine needles. I'm afraid to breathe.

The man goes to the car parked on the road, unlocks it and opens the boot. He hauls something out and struggles back up the bank and into the forest – he has a large stone. He places it where he's dug the hole then picks up the spade and looks around again even though it must be too dark for him to see much of anything. The possum in the tree above me grunts as I shift my weight from one foot to the other and the man whips around with the sound. He's staring right at me. I stay perfectly still. There's nothing else I can do.

Finally, he walks back to the car, still stumbling, and places the spade in the boot. As he drives off, slowly and carefully so the gravel is not disturbed, I think of a mnemonic to remember his licence plate number.

PCH990. *Peter's Cats Have 990 lives.*

The stone is heavy but not impossible for me to lift. It's a river stone, maybe from further up the road. There is a river in a gorge, a steep drop from the forestry, but the road drops down to it and crosses a concrete bridge. The stone is not out of place in the pine forest, but it would be difficult to find one like it. The perfect marker perhaps? I carry the stone to another tree, still six trees in from the road, but another six along to the right if you are facing the road. *Six and six. Peter's Cats Have 990 lives.* I walk back to where the stone was and cover the ground with more pine needles. The man has not made a very good job.

TWO

My name is Viola, not like the flower, the poor cousin of the showy pansy, but like the musical instrument. My mother plays the viola, and I am learning. Most days its rich, mellow notes fill our house – the dark, empty spaces full of sound. My mother is occasionally asked to play in the New Zealand Symphony Orchestra when one of their regular viola players is sick or overseas. It means she is away sometimes. It's difficult for me to go with her.

I wake each day, when dusk is already here, and lie listening to my mother play. Bach's melodies or Strauss' *Don Quixote* lift me out of bed. The quick bow work and her nimble fingers make me envious, and I work at stretching my own fingers so, one day, I too will be able to reach all the fingerings and maybe have the chance to play in an orchestra, like my mother. I want to hear the music swell and grow around me into some wild, enormous being before it swirls past the conductor to the auditorium and out into the world beyond. Of course I will have to change my name. Viola can't play the viola – everyone will laugh about it behind my back. I will change my name to Isabella or Charlotte or Clare without the 'i'.

One day, if there is to be a one day in the future for me.

I have Xeroderma Pigmentosum, or XP for short. Most complicated and deadly things it seems have abbreviations. My body is missing a vital gene that stops sunlight, UV light in particular (ultraviolet – another abbreviation – I know), from damaging my DNA (Deoxyribonucleic acid), which makes me who I am. Lots of things damage DNA, like smoking cigarettes and drinking alcohol and doing drugs, but most of the time bodies can repair the damage. With XP, the body can't. The damage is irreversible and it adds up. There are only about a thousand of us XP kids in the world. Few make it into adulthood. However careful we are, we always slip up sometime and the sun burns our flesh in seconds. It starts with blistering and then our skin ages and wrinkles. We develop skin cancers and they metastasise quickly, before anyone realises, and they grow into our vital organs and then we die.

My pale skin is already marked with freckles and moles, even though my parents have been so careful. The sun shining through a window or a bare fluorescent light bulb switched on damages it in seconds. Normal light bulbs are okay, but if I want to go out in daylight, I have to rub maximum protection sun block into my skin and even then still wear gloves and long pants and always socks and shoes and hats with cloths that cover my face so only my sunglasses can be seen. When I was young, Mum used to dress me up like this and take me into Ashburton, take me shopping with her and to the playground. I hated it. The clothes made me hot, and everywhere we went people would laugh at me, or point, or stare. It made me mad. Now I'm older I don't let her take me anywhere in the day. Now I only go outside at night, like vampires and werewolves. Anyway, it's safer that way.

They call kids with XP *moon children*. It's better than an abbreviation.

We live beside a forest in the Canterbury foothills. It is not a real forest. It's planted. As I have grown, so have the trees, and now we are both tall. They are Pinus radiata, or radiata pines as we call them, from California, and they are strong and straight, their branches pruned from them almost all the way up their rough trunks. The dead pine needles lie thick on the ground underneath, so little else grows. The trees march in lines; only a narrow slit of dark sky can be seen between, and a star or two, if they happen to fall there.

The forest is my playground, my territory. My parents believe it's safe. No one lives there; no one goes there at night, usually, except for me. One day, it will be logged and replanted with seedlings, which won't even come up to the top of my legs. For both of us, our days are numbered.

Although the waving pines let little light down to my level, I still only enter the forest when the sun is gone, when it's dark, just in case. At the third row I usually stop and listen to what the trees have to tell me about their day – whether a soft breeze is lifting their needles way up high or a wild nor'wester is smashing against them. Sometimes frost is settling on their tips, icy dancers sprinkling their magic.

But now I have to get home. Watching the car fire and the man dig his hole has taken up my evening. My mother expects me back before midnight, midnight at the very latest. She wants me inside and safe on my laptop, doing my school work or watching a movie before she goes to bed. She tries to protect me, even though she knows I am going to die anyway, one day soon.

I run. Whatever the man with the dreadlocks has buried will have to wait. The pine needles slip under my feet, the sticky sap from the trees wet on my fingertips. The house finally stands out in a white glare against the dark emptiness of the garden and paddocks. My mother doesn't bother leaving the back door light on for me. She knows what the house looks like with night vision. My parents both tried the goggles, after they gave them to me, to see what they were like. My father uses them occasionally when he goes possum or rabbit shooting, although he says the spotlight works just as well – the animal caught dazzled in the bright light giving him time to aim and shoot. Usually I go with him, holding his gun while he drives the four-wheel motorbike, me clinging onto the back over the bumps of the paddock, jumping off to open gates. The possums spread TB (another deadly abbreviation), which is a lung disease that used to kill people before there were antibiotics. As well as eating dope plants, possums also eat native bush. The rabbits eat the grass the sheep are meant to eat, and their burrows make holes in the paddocks. That's why we have to kill them both.

The farm does not make us a lot of money. Wool prices are low, and although everyone keeps saying they are getting better, they never really do. My dad says once, in the fifties, you could buy a new car with just one bale of wool. Farmers paid for their farms in two or three seasons of shearing. Now, clothes and carpet are made from recycled plastic milk containers, or corn husks, not wool from a sheep's back.

We make what we can by selling the lambs to the freezing works each autumn. They are slaughtered and cut up and packaged for sale in supermarkets in England and France, but the market is small. Americans eat beef steaks and beef burgers and beef tacos, and many Asians find our sheep meat too fatty, so we can only really sell to the Europeans, who are very good at growing their own roast lamb.

On the Canterbury Plains by the sea, and in the river valleys, the farmers make lots of money milking cows. Huge herds. A thousand cows or more. I've seen the irrigators the few times we've gone to Ashburton, driving at night. The long metal frames spray water onto the pastures even in the darkness, rotating slowly around the paddocks on their rubber wheels. We can't milk cows on our farm. There is not enough water and the grass isn't good enough. This is sheep country. And rabbit country and possum country. It grows good Californian pine trees.

My mother has been reading by the fire in the living room. She is ready for bed, in her pyjamas and dressing gown and sheepskin slippers. She closes the back door behind me, watching as I carefully pack the night-vision goggles into their case. I know she worries about me. There is no mobile phone reception on the farm or in the forest. No way for me to call for help if I need it before sunrise.

'What have you been up to?' she asks. 'It's almost midnight.'

'Just walking.' I take extra time closing the goggles case, my back to her, while I tell the lie. If I told her about the fat man burning, about how I followed the man with the dreadlocks through the forest, about how I moved the stone, what would she say? What would she do? I know she would get upset, and I know it would be the last time she ever allowed me out at night. There's no reason to tell her.

'I saw a possum,' I say.

'When you're old enough to get a gun licence you can take the gun with you.'

You have to be sixteen to get a gun licence in New Zealand, and I'm not counting on making it to sixteen. Mum really has no idea. Anyway, who is going to check on whether I have a gun licence or not when I'm out alone in the dark?

15

She goes to bed. Dad is already asleep. Farmers get up early. It's in their blood, Mum says. The only time I have ever seen Dad stay up late is to watch a rugby game on TV. Upstairs in my bedroom, I turn on my laptop and check my emails, my heart still thumping in my chest from what I have seen, what I have done. Laptops have LCD screens that don't give off UV light, so I'm okay. LCD stands for liquid crystal display, which is one of the few cool things I know that has an abbreviation. I keep in touch by email with some kids who have XP. One is in Australia and the rest are in the United States. We don't do webcams. Email is email, no one can see you, your odd pale face, the scars from the removed skin cancers, and you can think about what you say before you hit the send button. Anyway, it's night at different times around the world so hooking up at the same time is difficult. But tonight there are no emails from the XP kids, only one from my correspondence teacher, explaining where I went wrong in a maths problem.

Even if I didn't have XP, I would probably still learn by correspondence. It's a long way from where we live to the nearest school. My teacher drives out the hour or so from Ashburton to see me every couple of months. She laughs that it is easy to 'fit me in around all her other pupils' as she sees them during the day. Then she makes vampire and werewolf jokes.

I usually get through all my lessons by two in the morning and then just read or search the internet, eating what Mum has left out for me. I wander around online wherever I feel like going. Sometimes I end up in some really weird stuff but most of the time it's okay. I'm not dumb. My parents can trust me. And my teacher has that software that picks up when you've copied and pasted words straight off the net, so there's no cheating.

By first light I'm watching music videos or TV on the internet, and then it's time for bed.

But tonight I'm entering the licence plate number of the car the man drove off in into a car licensing website I've finally found. PCH990 is a brand new silver Toyota Camry. To get the owner's name I have to pay. My parents gave me, for my last birthday, my own debit card. They put fifty dollars on it every month as 'pocket money'. It is perfect for getting things online. The report comes up instantly. The silver Camry was bought by Samuel Baker of Ashburton from a car dealer. He is the legal owner.

Car fires, I find out on another site, are usually caused by electrical faults and leaky fuel lines. Both can be found under the bonnet. If the fuel line is leaking because it is old and cracked, or deliberately damaged, a spark from the engine starting can ignite the fumes from the fuel. Car fires are also very hot because cars are made of flammable materials like plastic and whatever is in the seat stuffing, and then there is the fuel tank and the battery. They can be so hot that the metal buckles. But not so hot that bodies inside are completely burnt, not beyond all recognition. The human body is made up of too much water for that to happen. Unless, of course, there is more accelerant added to the fire, like extra containers of petrol. Then there can be nothing left.

Three

The day after I was born, when I was barely twenty-four hours old, my mother took me outside. She had been in hospital all that day, and the day before that, and the day before that in labour with me, so she wanted to fill her lungs with fresh air, feel the wind on her face, the sun on her skin again. And she wanted me to feel it, too, for the very first time. She wanted to show me the world. All of it, all at once. The nurses told her off for not wrapping me up warmly enough, even though it was a summer's day, so she went back to our room and got a white lamb's wool shawl my grandmother had knitted in expectation. Then, evading the nurses this time, she walked out of the hospital doors, me in her arms.

Wrapped in that shawl, only my face was exposed

and one hand that I had somehow managed to pull free. The sun was behind a cloud. My mother walked down the steps of the hospital, past the cars in the car park and out onto the street. She was away, at last, from hospital smells and the stuffy closed rooms where the windows wouldn't open. No longer was there carpet or vinyl under her feet. Instead there was the earth and grass. She carried me, and my eyes were open, and I was looking up at everything – the trees, the blue sky, clouds, birds flying high above us. And then the sun came out.

Instantly my back arched, my body taut, my tiny fingers reaching out to the golden object in the sky, and I screamed.

My mother, terrified, turned and ran back to the hospital as fast as she could, but it was too late. The skin on my face and my miniature hand was already blistering.

That's how they found out I had XP.

I can remember none of this. Even children can remember few things, if anything, from before they are the age of three. My mother has told me what happened, explained it to me many times as I was growing up and trying to understand. I asked different questions when I was five, when I was seven, and now that I am fourteen.

They always answer the same way, my parents – my

20

father's voice silent, my mother's voice full of words of care.

Both of my parents are genetic carriers of XP. I had a one-in-four chance of not being a carrier and not having the condition, a one-in-two chance of being a carrier but not having the condition, and a one-in-four chance of being a carrier *and* having the condition. One in four, a twenty-five per cent probability, one quarter – they all mean the same thing. I was unlucky.

My doctor at Ashburton Hospital explained it to me, drawing it on paper. Everyone else gets to study this in school, in science. Me, I got to learn it earlier – it was my life lesson. There was this guy, Gregor Mendel, who was a priest ages ago in Austria, in Europe, and he grew peas. He figured out certain things were inherited, like the colour of the flowers of the pea plant.

Imagine a square divided into four quarters. This square represents one gene. Along the top, label both parts 'A'. And down the left-hand side, label both parts 'A' as well. These are the parents.

For each gene, half comes from the father and half from the mother. If you multiply the box out, all four segments will have 'AA' in them. These are possible children. The parents and their kids are all the same for this particular gene. If this is the XP gene, then 'AA' stands for normal, non-carrier, like almost everyone is.

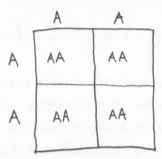

If you make one parent normal 'AA', and one a carrier 'Aa', then the box ends up with two 'AA's and two 'Aa's – two normal people and two carriers which is no big deal. Carriers don't have XP.

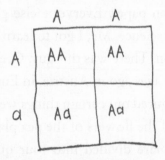

But if you make both parents carriers 'Aa', you get one 'AA', two 'Aa's and one 'aa'. That 'aa' is me. Someone with XP.

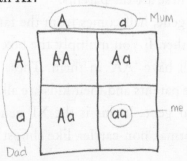

After I was born, and they found out they were both carriers, Mum and Dad decided not to have any more children. I was their first and I would be their last. They didn't want to roll the dice again, flip the coin, deal the cards, see what came out of Mendel's square this time. You might think that with me born, another child would only be a carrier or even totally okay – as long as they only had four children, one of them would be okay, two would be carriers, and there would be me, the unlucky one. But it doesn't work that way. If you flip a coin, there is a fifty-fifty chance it will be heads and a fifty-fifty chance it will be tails, and it's like that every time you flip it. Even if you flip that coin ninety-nine times and it always comes up heads, on the hundredth time there will still be only a fifty-fifty chance that it will be tails. Probability has no memory. It certainly doesn't care about anything either. It only has reasoning – logic. I try to be logical. It helps. Either that or I really am the unlucky one.

When I get up, my mother asks me if I know anything about a car catching fire on one of the forestry roads nearby. The police have been round earlier, knocking on the door and 'making inquiries'.

'A car fire?'

'That's right, last night,' she says, leaning back

against the kitchen bench watching me eat scrambled eggs. 'You would have told me, wouldn't you, when you came in last night, if you had seen anything?'

'I didn't see anything. Did you or Dad see anything?'

'No.'

'How did the police know about it? Did Dad find the car?'

'No. We never go up there, you know that. A forestry worker found it.'

The shovel from the woolshed is heavy to run with. I dart down the rows of trees towards the far road, the handle sometimes banging against a trunk when I am not careful. I have waited for complete darkness, just in case. The road is empty when I get there, and the river stone is the way I left it, grey on grey through the night-vision goggles. There's no sign that anyone has been here since last night. I count the trees back from the stone and start to dig. The man has made it easy. The ground is still soft and the shovel slips into it with little force. I pile the dirt carefully beside the hole, feeling for the bag with each push of the shovel between the tree roots.

There it is.

I reach down and use my hands, forcing the dirt aside and pull it up. The ground releases it slowly.

It's a black plastic rubbish bag, the handles tied at the top. I resist the temptation to tear the plastic apart and instead spend precious seconds untying the slippery knots. There are more plastic bags inside, all the same. I lift one out and look at it. The plastic is clear and inside are hundred-dollar notes. Lots of them.

I fill in the hole with the dirt, jump up and down a few times to make the ground hard, then spread the pine needles on top. No one would know a hole has been dug, and undug, and filled back up. I take the rubbish bag and the shovel and I run.

I think about the fat man, stuffed behind the wheel of the burning car.

If the hundred-dollar notes are in bundles of ten, then each bundle is a thousand dollars. If they're in bundles of twenty, then each bundle is two thousand dollars. If they're in bundles of fifty, then it is five thousand dollars. How many bundles are in each bag?

I stop. I'm in the middle of the forest. It's quiet. There's no wind, no sound of the branches shifting, scraping together, needles falling. I'm alone, like I always am in the forest, but now I look around carefully to make sure. There's nothing but tall, straight pines. I take two steps backwards so I can look past the closest tree. The vertical lines rearrange themselves in the night-vision goggles. Still nothing.

I open the bag again.

There are one hundred hundred-dollar notes in each bundle. I count them carefully. The picture of the man with the droopy moustache is on every note – Rutherford, the scientist from Nelson who went to England about a hundred years ago and won the Nobel Prize for splitting the atom. So that's ten thousand dollars in each bundle. There are ten bundles in each bag, so that's one hundred thousand dollars. I count the bundles twice to make sure, laying them out on the pine needles, before returning them to the clear plastic bag. The clear bags are those ones with the sliding tops that seal them. I take them all out of the rubbish bag, and lay them out in rows of five to make sure I count them right. There are two rows. That's ten small bags, each of one hundred thousand. I figure out the maths, counting the zeros. My correspondence teacher would be proud of me. There is one zero in ten, and five in one hundred thousand, so that's six zeros. I can do the maths, but the number is too big to stick in my head, or maybe I'm too excited, too scared. I sweep the pine needles off the ground and write the numbers in the dry dirt with my finger, adding the commas. I count the zeros again. I'm right. It's a million dollars.

I sweep away the numbers in the dirt, then pile back the pine needles, throw all the bags of money into the rubbish bag and tie the handles together again, pick it and the shovel up, and run.

A million dollars that belonged to a fat man who got burnt up in a car fire and a dope grower who must have killed him for the money and now I have it and no one knows.

No one knows.

My owl is squatting on a tree branch up ahead. I can see his eyes. In the night-vision goggles they look different to a possum's. He's not really my owl, but I see him most nights, so he has become mine, my night guardian. He's a morepork, New Zealand's native owl. They're called moreporks because that's the sound they make when they're calling out in the dark. My owl is watching me run down the rows of trees carrying a shovel and a rubbish bag full of a million dollars in one-hundred dollar notes. He has his own, built-in, night-vision goggles.

He knows.

When the weather is bad, too bad to go into the forest, I go to the woolshed and practise the viola. I can't play it late at night in the house, as it will wake up Dad. You can get a practice mute, which fits onto the bridge of the viola and muffles the sound, but Mum doesn't believe in them. You need to work on your bowing technique and with a mute you won't be able to hear what you are doing wrong, she says. So I take my viola out into the woolshed. I turn on all the lights. They're normal bulbs, not fluorescents, so I'm safe. I sit on the edge of the shearing board, where the shearers shear the sheep, and practise what my mother taught me earlier in the evening. Sometimes, I stand on the shearing board and play, pretending it is a stage and the bales of wool on the concrete floor below are my audience. I set my music up where the shearers keep their spare combs and their cutters by the sheep pen doors, and I play to the bales and the spiders and the brooms left scattered by the shed hands.

The wood of the shearing board is polished smooth with lanolin from the sheep's wool – each sheep is dragged on its back by the shearer the half metre from the holding pens to the shearing plant, and this has worn away at the wood. Thousands of sheep, their annual coats being cut from them by the noisy machines, have been sat here. Then they are nudged over to the chutes, which land them back outside onto the grass as if nothing has happened – except for a few cuts and bruises, and a missing coat, that is. Once, a sheep got stuck behind the chute and they had to cut the floor of the shearing board out to get at it. Instead of nailing the floor up again they just slotted the cut boards back, in case they had to get another stuck sheep out. But it hasn't happened again. That I know of.

That's where I'll hide the bag.

The woolshed is dark and empty when I slip inside. I don't turn on the lights, just in case my mother pulls her bedroom curtains aside and looks out into the night, wondering why she can't hear the faint notes of music. Once the first board is out, the rest are simple. I have to push the bag into the space though. It's too fat, just like the sheep once was. That's how it had got stuck, my father told me. I pummel the bag and finally it fits into the space between the chute and the wall.

I replace the boards. They look just like they did before. My hiding place won't be found.

Jim, in his kennel, watches as I run between the woolshed and the house. He is the oldest of the sheep dogs and my favourite. He's sitting the way he always does, with his front paws crossed. He was a puppy when I was little. Dad says he trained us together to work the sheep. Unlike the rest of the dogs, which are black and tan, Jim is golden with a white chest and four paws and his eyes are different colours. One brown like a normal dog's but the other is blue. He can still see out of it but it makes him look weird. Mum calls him a clown dog.

Jim yawns and I tell him to go back to sleep. Old dogs need their sleep. He doesn't need to look out for me.

It's almost midnight. I have maths homework to do. More maths. The last few hours of my night vanish in school work and on the net.

When I get up the next night my mother has the newspaper open on the kitchen table. The sun has barely set. I'm reminded again how my nights are getting shorter as the weather warms, the sun lingering longer and longer in the sky above the Southern Alps.

'See the story at the bottom of the page,' she says. She's poaching me two eggs. Sometimes it's scrambled eggs for breakfast, sometimes it's poached, sometimes it's no eggs at all but leftovers from whatever they had for tea or lunch. We have our own chickens so eggs are always in the fridge, even when we have run out of almost everything else. The supermarket isn't just round the corner. Mum only goes once a month.

'What story?'

'Have a look.' She points to the bottom of the left-hand page of the newspaper. 'Remember I asked you about that fire yesterday? How the police came? Appears there was a body in the car.'

I casually read the story and look at the photo next to it, trying to show little interest.

'So?'

'It's just awful. Someone ending up like that. Awful. And so close to here.'

I shrug my shoulders and wish the eggs would cook a little faster. I get my vitamin D capsules out of the cupboard. I have to take one every day because vitamin D is the one vitamin you get from exposure to the sun, and I can't have anything of me exposed to the sun. Without vitamin D, my bones won't grow properly and could break. There are foods that have vitamin D in them, such as milk and eggs (mine are still cooking), but there are only so many eggs I can eat.

'Nice looking man too,' Mum says. 'A nice smile. I wish we had known; we could have done something. We're the closest house to where it happened.'

'How do they know who was in the car?' I ask, indifferent.

'You haven't read the story properly. It was his car and he's missing so it must be him. Usually they check things like dental records but apparently his teeth were all broken. They think that's how he was murdered. He was hit in the head. They think there were extra fuel containers in the car, for it to burn like it did.'

'Oh.' I look at the photo again, of Geoff Harris, 37, of Ashburton. He's not the fat man. He's the man who buried the money. The man with the dreadlocks. He's even wearing a bandana in the photo, just like he was when he was burning the fat man in the car.

'So, I suppose the police will be looking for who murdered him.'

'Yes. You sure you didn't see anything?' she asks again. 'I'd hate to think you were out there when something like that was happening.'

'I didn't see anything.'

'Car fires are pretty noisy. Well, I suppose they are. They are on TV. The fuel tank explodes. Tyres explode. If you were in the forestry you would have heard at least a couple of loud bangs.'

'No.'

'You wouldn't have known what it was.'

'I didn't hear anything. I didn't see anything. All right?'

32

Four

I'm playing the viola in the living room with my mother listening. I'm still silently angry with her for asking me again about the car fire. She's watching the notes on the sheet of paper on the music stand from over my shoulder. She points to the bar I've just stuffed up. I stop and go back, but she interrupts me again.

'You're gripping the bow too tightly. Loosen up your hand,' she instructs.

I try to do what she says, starting again.

'To get that big sound, don't expect your fingers to do it. That is what your arm is for. Use the weight of your arm.'

I try again, but my body now feels even more rigid. One of the hairs on the bow breaks and waves around.

'Just pull it off.' Mum stops me again.

I grab the piece of horse hair and pull it from the tip of the bow.

'Now play.'

The music at last swirls around me, calms me. It's *Meditation* by Jules Massenet. He's a nineteenth-century French composer and *Meditation* is one of his best-known works. Mum likes Massenet because she says he composed his music in his imagination, not sitting at a piano tinkering. He never used to go to performances of his work either. He was too afraid. He asked people who had been in the audience how it had gone, what they had thought of it.

I like Massenet because he was a soldier in the Franco-Prussian War. Not many composers were soldiers too.

The music is making the curtains covering the living room windows dance, or seem to, but it will be the easterly blowing outside. One of the windows must be slightly open.

I think I am good, for my age, for the number of years I have been playing, but I have no way of knowing. My mother corrects me lots but never praises me. I asked her once if I was any good, but she never answered. Not with an answer that meant anything. Most kids who learn a musical instrument take exams with the Associated Board of the Royal Schools of Music or with Trinity Guildhall London. The examiners come out every year to New Zealand and grade pupils – pass, merit, distinction. There are theory exams on Saturday mornings, questions to answer on sheets of paper from England about how music is written (What is a treble clef? What is the timing of a piece of music?). My mother has her fellowship (FTCL) from Trinity in the performance of music framed in the hallway. It is the highest level you can achieve.

I am not sure why she doesn't put me forward for the examinations. I found the syllabuses on the internet and some of the music I've learnt to play is listed in them. The exams are in Ashburton, and I know it is difficult for me to get there, but it's not impossible. Maybe the examiners will not work at night. Maybe they will not make an exception for me and hold the exam in a room with no fluorescent lights, or have a supervisor watch me sit a theory exam all by myself, at night.

Or maybe I am not good enough to pass and my mother knows this, which is why she does not enter me.

When I finish playing the final, soft, long note she says nothing as usual. I pack the viola carefully into its case, cover it with the cloth as she taught me, and put the bow in the space for it in the lid. I know which parts of the music I need to practise more, and then, when

I have it right and can play the whole piece, I will start on the next one Mum gives me.

She seems to have forgotten about the car fire, because she asks me what I am going to do for the rest of the night. I was worried she might not let me out into the forest now she knows how close death has come.

'I might go for a walk,' I say, carefully.

'Keep safe,' she says and turns back into the kitchen, the evening dishes still to do, the bread dough to be made so it can rise overnight.

It is not unusual for my mother to feel responsible for things she can do nothing about, wanting to protect a life that is close to her own – if you can call about three kilometres of gravel forestry road close. I mean, what could she have done to save the fat man's life? He was already dead before the fire started, killed in Ashburton or somewhere else, his teeth bashed in. Geoff Harris was just using the forestry road to get rid of the body. He probably didn't even know he was close to a farm, a house. He definitely didn't know he was being watched. And when he comes back to dig up his money, maybe he'll just think the stone has been moved accidentally, or that he put it by the wrong tree in the dark or something. Really, I don't care what he thinks. I have his million dollars. The fat man's million dollars. It must be drug money. Geoff Harris is a dope grower. I know that. I saw him. It must be drug money. Drug money is finders keepers. It's my money now.

But I can't tell my mother, or Dad because he would tell her even if I asked him not to. Mum rescues baby birds, has new-born lambs in cardboard boxes by the fire in the living room to warm up, saves worms that have wiggled on to the concrete path outside the house from drying out in the sun. What would she think if she knew her daughter watched a car burn with someone inside it and did nothing?

I wonder sometimes, how my mother survives on the farm, where we kill possums and rabbits, and send lambs to the freezing works once a year – the same lambs that only months ago she had by the fire. Dad will butcher a sheep for us to eat – grabbing it in the yards, cutting its throat so it bleeds out, then, hanging it – dead and still – by its back legs, pulling off the skin with its fleece, taking the guts out, and a day later, once the meat has set, chopping it into four roasts and twenty-four chops with the farm dogs getting the rest. But Mum will never watch, never help. Dad let me kill my first sheep last year. It's all about technique he said, not strength.

When I was younger, Dad used to do a lot of the farm work at night. He wanted to spend time with me, show me what he did each day, and the only way to do that safely for me was after dark. We would shift the sheep, go round the lambing mobs, bring them in to treat them for flystrike, put the rams out. It was okay. He even had the shearing gangs come at night for a while. They would spend four days shearing the ewes and the hoggets and the rams. I learned how to pick up a fleece and throw it on the table, skirt the edges and separate the bellies, the neck, the top knot, sweep the board clean for the shearer between each sheep. Mum would cook a big meal for the shearers and the wool handlers and the presser and serve it up at midnight. The shearing gang did it for two years then they refused the next. It was too tough on them, getting back into a day routine afterwards, they said. Even though we were paying them more, enough was enough.

Dad doesn't do so much of the farm work at night, now that I'm older. If there's a big job and he needs me, like the drenching, he'll sometimes wait until dusk and we'll go out together, but most of the time now he does the farm work during the day. The dogs work better then, he says. The sheep can't see that well at night, they can get packed up in the corners of the paddocks, smothered against the fences, because they can't see the open gateway.

When I walk to where the burning car was, it's gone. Police tape and a dark spot where the flames scorched the gravel are the only signs of what has happened. I touch the police tape. The easterly has blown it into the trees and it has threaded itself around the trunks. Something foreign, unneeded, unnecessary. Why did they put up police tape? Who would cross it? Who was around to do that, even when the burnt-out car was still here? The plastic is smooth between my fingers. I want to get rid of it, take it away from fouling up this place. The tape is rubbish that should be disposed of, not left to blow into the forest. But if I take it back to the farm, Mum will know I have been here.

I leave the tape tangled in the trees.

Where have the remains of the car gone? There was nothing much left of the fat man, according to the newspaper, but there was enough left of the car to identify it. Had a licence plate escaped the heat?

I turn away from the road and the police tape blowing in the wind and walk through the forest. The boot marks and signs of people only reach four rows of trees in. The police should have searched for clues of what happened, whether anyone had left on foot after the fire. They should have had sniffer dogs to help them find a scent. They should have been searching for reasons why the car had been destroyed, why a body was in it. Maybe they didn't have enough people to do a proper search, or the dogs, or the time.

My morepork flies through the trees above me, his wings outstretched, almost touching the branches. Silent. It is out hunting in the dark.

Where the bag was buried is just the way I left it. The stone further over is unmoved. I get down on my hands and knees and study the ground in the white-green glow through the night-vision goggles. There is no sign that anybody has been here in the past day.

I consider myself a pretty good tracker. I've read about Daniel Boone and Buffalo Bill, and about how Aborigines find their way through Australian deserts. I know what to look for, what is important. And I can do it myself. I've practised lots. And I can do it in the dark, which I don't think Daniel Boone and Buffalo Bill ever did. There aren't a lot of wild animals here, not ones that stay on the ground anyway, except for wild pigs, and I try to keep my distance from them – so I've tracked myself. I leave something, a hat or a scarf, and head off walking, taking no notice of where I am, until I hit a road or a fence line that I know. Then I retrace my steps. It's not easy. I mean, you can make it easy by scuffing up the pine needles and bending back branches, but I don't cheat. I make it hard. And I can do it, although there was one scarf I didn't find for a couple of months, and even then it was by accident. Mum wasn't impressed when I brought it in to be washed. A winter's worth of rain hadn't done it much good.

I check the gravel road too, for signs of cars that may have stopped, footprints in the dirt on the side of the road, bent stalks in the long grass. Again there is nothing.

When will he come back for his million dollars?

When will he find out it's gone?

Will the cops come back with dogs that will lead them from the blackened road to the river stone and then to the woolshed?

I look up and down the gravel road, suddenly wary. There is nothing. No sound. Nothing. An empty road, pine trees moving in the wind, stars.

I retreat into the forest, sit down a little way off from the stone where it should be and wait, just in case. The cold, in the end, drives me home.

Mum has already gone to bed. I find the newspaper and read the article about the car fire again. Thinking, I turn to the back of the paper, to the classifieds, where the death notices are. I look down the column. His is near the top – they're listed alphabetically.

HARRIS, *Geoffrey Thomas (Geoff) of Ashburton – aged 37 years. Loved and only son of the late Ngaire and Thomas Harris, much*

*loved brother and brother-in-law of Sarah and
Ben Davies (Sydney) and adored by his young
nephews Peter and Nicholas. A memorial service
to celebrate Geoff's life will be held on Tuesday
at 3 p.m. at the Ashburton Funeral Chapel,
corner of East and Cox Streets, Ashburton.*

But he's not dead. I saw him, running through the trees.
I saw him bury the bag full of money.

Five

The bank manager came today. He's really called a Rural Lending Specialist (I've seen his business card) but Dad calls him the bank manager. He visits about every six months, to eat lunch and to talk about the money his bank gives us so we can continue farming. I'm always asleep when he's here so I've never met him, but I always know when he's coming, and when he's gone. Beforehand, Mum cleans the whole house and searches through cookbooks for what to make him for lunch. Dad puts the best looking sheep in the paddock by the front gate. Afterwards, the smell of aftershave lingers in the dining room, and the reflections of my parent's faces caught against the darkened windows always look worried.

When they turn to me, when they realise that I'm

there, they smile with an 'everything will be all right, you're too young to understand, to know, to worry' smile. But I'm not that young. I understand.

Tonight, I sit on the third-bottom step of the stairs and listen through the open crack of the living-room door. They don't know that I'm up yet. Dad is talking.

'You know they can't sell them all at once?'

He waits for an answer. Mum must have nodded because he continues.

'If they called in every loan on everyone like us they would have so many farms to sell there would be a glut in the market. The price of farmland would crash. The banks wouldn't get their money back. That's why they do it just a few at a time. And I don't think we're at the top of their list. There are a lot of farmers in a lot worse situation than we are.'

'I know,' I hear Mum whisper.

'We've just got to keep doing what we do best. The bank knows we're good farmers. They know that what's happening is not our fault. We can't control the interest rates and the US dollar, the price of diesel. The council rates. How much did they go up this year? We're doing our best, and that's what we've got to keep on doing.'

'I know.'

Mum will be sitting on the sofa, my father standing by the fire. Mum will be looking at the floor, like she

44

does, but her eyes won't be seeing the worn carpet. She just won't want to look at Dad and his grim determination and his hope that they can carry on as they have always carried on.

I don't know how much money my parents borrowed from the bank when they bought the farm. I do know it's called a mortgage. And then there is the overdraft which is for the daily working expenses. Sheep farmers only get paid a few times a year. Once when we send the lambs to the works after Christmas, and once for the wool we shear off them and their mothers. But, every month, money is going out to pay the council rates, and to pay for fertiliser and for diesel for the tractor and for drench to keep the sheep healthy and for Mum to go to the supermarket. Then there's the bank's interest to pay too. Interest is what the bank charges us to use their money. It's a percentage of the money owed. What percentage the bank charges as interest depends on the OCR (the official cash rate – yes, I know, yet another abbreviation) which is the interest rate set by the Reserve Bank which is like the big bank of New Zealand. The Reserve Bank uses the OCR to control inflation. Inflation is rising prices which is bad for economic stability. From what I've figured out, using the OCR doesn't work too well. Every time farmers get more for their lambs or their milk or their wool it puts more money into the economy, which raises inflation so the Reserve Bank puts the OCR up so we have to pay more in interest to the banks. We don't get ahead at all. The OCR just keeps farmers in debt.

Anyway, the lamb cheque and the wool cheque goes into the overdraft once a year and is supposed to clear it, take it back to zero and leave a bit besides, to pay off the mortgage so there will be less interest to pay next year. But some years that doesn't happen. When it doesn't happen, the debt in the overdraft is transferred to the mortgage, so the mortgage gets bigger and there is more interest to pay. If the mortgage gets bigger than the value of the farm, or the interest gets more than what we could ever pay in a year, then the bank will take the farm off us and sell it and we will get nothing. We will have to leave. Find somewhere else to live. Somewhere in a city.

I think this is how it all happens. That's what I've read on the internet, and in the farming newspapers that Dad leaves lying around. I've studied percentages in maths. A percentage of a small amount of money is not a lot, like ten per cent off an ebook which only costs a few dollars, but ten per cent on hundreds of thousands, perhaps millions of dollars, is a lot of money, a lot of lambs, a lot of wool.

'Viola should be awake,' I hear Mum say through

the door, but there is no sound of movement in the room. I count to ten, the only sound I can hear is my own breathing, then I carefully get up and step back to the fifth stair, which always creaks.

'There she is,' Mum says. 'Viola, we're in here,' she calls out.

I bound down the last few stairs and push open the door to the living room, remembering to pull down the sleeve of my jersey just in time. There is a sore, a redness, on the back of my arm near my wrist, which I noticed for the first time when I woke. It could be a skin cancer, a melanoma. It could be nothing. When I went out a few weeks ago, it was still daylight, just; the sun was setting, and maybe there was a gap between my gloves and my jacket that I didn't notice. I don't know. And I don't want Mum to know.

'Morning,' Mum says, smiling. 'About time you got up.'

'I had lots of school work to do last night. Morning, Dad.'

The 'morning' thing is our evening ritual. I'm not sure if it's to amuse them, or me, but it's stuck. Our family joke, our way of dealing with me having XP. One of the XP kids I email in the States said they do it, too, in her family. So we're not the only crazy ones. Mum goes into the kitchen to start my breakfast. Dad talks about the sheep, how the tailing gang are coming. No one mentions the bank manager, or money, or having to leave the farm, but I can smell the aftershave in the air.

The trees welcome me as usual. The night is clear, a frost in the making. A late winter frost, maybe the last one of the year. I like the frost. It makes me feel privileged – I'm one of the few people in the world who watches its magic unfold. Almost everyone else wakes up in the morning and it is there, on the ground, on the fences, on the trees, but I see it slowly form, ice crystal upon ice crystal, whiteness upon whiteness.

As I walk I can just hear the murmur of the river, the one the logging road crosses. On clear, still nights like this you can sometimes hear it through the trees. It is a braided river, the many channels rush past gravel banks and around islands and large rocks, rejoining then splitting apart again. The gravel and the rocks have been washed down from the mountains during snow melt, and when westerly storms pound them with rain. Most of the rivers in Canterbury are braided. This is an eroding landscape, a landscape still in the making.

I don't go near the river. It's a steep drop. I don't know, maybe thirty or forty metres from the forest floor, and at the edge the pine needles are slippery.

Once you start heading down that slope there's only one way you are going to go.

I keep the sound of the river on my right side and ignore it calling to me.

Where the stone is, and where the money was, is still undisturbed. Nothing has changed since last night or the night before that or the night before that. I sit down to watch, to see if the man will come back, and think about the sore on my arm and what I should do about it. I probably know more about melanomas and what they look like than most doctors and nurses. I google, and I get checked out all the time by my doctor who I have an appointment with every six months, and I watch my skin for any signs. This one doesn't look good. It could be a basal cell carcinoma, which is relatively harmless and just needs to be cut out, or it could be a full-on melanoma and the cancer is already spreading to my lymph nodes. I have no way of knowing, so, really, it's not worth thinking about. I don't want Mum to fuss.

After about half an hour of just sitting and watching, it gets too cold. I need to move to keep warm. And anyway, I think I know what I'm going to do.

The house is a white glow in the night-vision goggles, the frost on the lawn is already crunchy underfoot. Mum, in her dressing gown and with book in hand, comes up to me as I take off my jacket and pack the night-vision goggles into their case in the laundry.

'You're cold,' she says, as she gives me a quick hug.

'There's a frost.'

'So that's why you've come in early. Won't be too many more, hopefully. Spring is almost here.' Her voice sounds dull, flat, her thoughts probably still on the bank manager's visit.

'Yeah,' I say, as I close the lid of the case carefully.

'Good night then,' she says and turns away.

'Mum, is it okay if I get some paper out of the office? Just need to print out some assignments, for school.'

'Of course.'

I don't need to turn the light on. I know my way around in the half light of the moon coming in through the office windows, their curtains unpulled. I tug a few pages from an opened packet of paper by the printer, then quietly pull open the top drawer of the desk where the envelopes are kept and grab one, hiding it in the paper in my arms.

'Good night,' my mother calls softly from her bedroom door on the landing as I head up the stairs, the fifth one creaking on cue.

'Good night, Mum.'

Bedroom doors are closed, everything is fine, is normal.

I switch on the light and study the envelope. It is

white, rectangular, sized to hold A4 sheets of paper folded neatly into three. There are no marks on it, nothing special about it. It's the type that arrives regularly in our mailbox, as, I suppose, in mailboxes everywhere. It's perfect.

In my bedroom, I turn on my laptop and hook it up to its little printer, find the envelope printing function but then stop, not knowing what to type. Should I put my parent's names on it? Address it like a letter? Then they would know whoever has done it must know them, or know of them. Then they would be worried. But if the envelope was just blank they probably would take it to the police, thinking it wasn't theirs. That someone had left it there by mistake. I type in my parents' names and then add 'please use wisely' and quickly print the envelope. The printer grabs it and stuffs it through its innards before spitting it out, task accomplished. I check the result. It could have been printed by any of thousands of printers. There is nothing to connect it to me.

Except my finger prints, but I'll wipe them off before I put the envelope in our mailbox.

Six

The next night nothing happens. I get up; my mother cooks me scrambled eggs and sausages; I practise the viola with her (Massenet again – I'll get the piece perfect one day); I go out into the forest and check the stone, see a possum run along the ground, go home, do school work, watch TV on the internet, go to bed.

Nothing happens.

The next night, the same.

The next night I want to ask, to scream, to just find out because my parents are saying nothing.

NOTHING.

I slam the door on the way out. They can think the wind has caught it. I adjust the night-vision goggles, zip up my jacket and stomp through the garden and out the back gate towards the trees. I mean how can they say nothing? What else don't they tell me? Okay, I accept them not saying stuff about the bank and paying the interest because they don't want me to worry and I don't care anyway because I understand it all but what else is going on that I don't know about?

A rabbit screeches in the night. A ferret must have it, pulling it from its burrow. I've seen it happen through the night-vision goggles, otherwise I wouldn't recognise the sound, wouldn't link it to the act. I ignore it, there is nothing I can do even if I wanted to. Well done ferret, now go and find some more. I enter the forest.

The branches are shuffling in the breeze. Pine needle on pine needle, chattering away to each other as if they have to talk about something, about the weather, about what a good day it's been, how the sun shone so nicely, so brightly, didn't it? It's noisy. It's so noisy I can't think. Why don't they all just shut up for once?

The walk to the stone seems to take longer than usual, the slight slope more uphill, the act of treading lightly on the pine needles so as to leave no track, harder to do. The breeze is getting stronger, the noise from the branches louder above me. I spot my morepork. He has something in its talons. He swoops overhead with the bloodied scrap clutched beneath it. Maybe he is off to his nest, to feed newly hatched young, or maybe he will feast alone. I don't know. And I don't care. No one tells me anything.

I'm nearing the road and I stop, looking. Someone has been here. Even from this distance I can tell. I skirt around the area and check the road, keeping within the safety of the trees. There's no car, but the marks of one are plain to see. Someone has spun the wheels, sprayed the gravel. Either they left in a hurry or they left in a rage. I go back to the stone. It has been hurled aside, the ground underneath dug furiously, the hole far bigger than should have been needed. All around the tree, holes have been dug, and around the next tree and many trees nearby. None have been filled in – the dirt flung far, the pine needles shoved aside. I gulp in air. The person who did this wasn't thinking rationally, they didn't carefully test the ground for a soft spot where the bag might have been. And they didn't try to hide that they were here. This person was angry. Angry and, in the end, desperate. I count the six trees back, keeping six from the road and find the spot where the bag had been buried. The spot is untouched.

I walk further into the forest, away from the road and the newly dug holes, further away than I have been sitting and watching. I crouch down and lean against a tree and think. Had the man come in daylight? Last night I left here about 11pm so sometime between then and now (I check my watch – it's 9.45pm) he came. If he came in the dark and couldn't find the bag he might think it was just because he was in the wrong place, that he had found the wrong stone. That the money was still there, somewhere, he just hadn't found where he had hidden it. The stone was a useless marker. There were too many around the same.

If he came in daylight to look, he would know that it really is gone.

Had he come to take the money away with him, or just to check that it was still there? Why would he come to check it was still there? He had no reason to believe anyone knew where it was, no reason to believe anyone had watched him bury it. He would have come to dig it up and take it away, to hide it somewhere else, or to spend it. Maybe he didn't take it the night of the fire in case someone stopped his car and searched it. Like the police or a fire crew. But that doesn't make sense. The car had burned to nothing on a deserted road in the middle of a forestry plantation. No one knew about it until the next day when a forestry worker found it. The driver of the car *Peter's Cats Have 999 lives* would have driven away safely. He must have buried the money because he had no place else to hide it. And now, a week and one day later, he does, but he can't find the money.

I don't watch any longer. I turn and run.

I have to practise the viola. I play Brahms' *Hungarian Dance Number One* standing on the shearing board in the woolshed, the instrument tucked under my chin. I try to focus on the sheet music propped up next to the sheep pen, but my eyes keep straying to the shadowed corners where the full wool bales are stacked, the dark empty sheep pens, the heavy metal door that clangs and clatters when you slide it open. The music falters; my memory of the piece isn't good enough, and I have to find my place and replay the bar. Over and over again, like a stuck record my mother would say, but I never know what she means by it. An old saying, she consoles me.

She will be in the house, reading her book by the fire, listening. She says she can hear me when I play in the woolshed. But maybe the wind tonight is too strong, the noise of it buffeting the house too loud. Maybe she won't hear if I suddenly stop and then don't come home. Maybe I'm not safe here at all.

The floor of the shearing board, where the cut pieces of wood are slotted back together, is beneath my feet. No one has been here. No one has touched anything. My body shifts with the music, the bow dictating my movements. I'm just a kid, practising her viola in the middle of the night in a woolshed on a Canterbury sheep farm. Nothing unusual at all. Nothing strange. Nothing for anyone to think twice about.

When my fingers go numb with cold, I sprint back to the house, my viola and bow in their case tucked under my arm. Jim, in his kennel, his paws crossed as always, watches me.

I nestle the plate of cheese toasties on my duvet cover and wish I had heeded my mother's warning about toast crumbs in the bed, but it's too late. A cup of hot chocolate has already warmed my hands so I can type. I google Geoff Harris, the man with the dreadlocks, the man who buried the money, the man whose life has just been celebrated by the mourners at the Ashburton Chapel. There is a Geoff Harris who is a racing car driver. There is a movie director, a visual arts moderator (whatever that is), a company board member and an amateur photographer. None of them look like the Geoff Harris I know. I google 'Geoff Harris Ashburton' and still there is nothing helpful. I look up the white pages and there are no listings for Geoff or Geoffrey Harris in Ashburton but there are twenty-two for G Harris. People very rarely put their first names as part of their phone listings and there is no reason to have your phone number listed at all.

I think how Geoff Harris had pulled the fat man from the car boot, dug the hole under the tree. He was fit and strong. Maybe he goes to a gym. Maybe he works as a builder so is used to digging and carrying heavy stuff. Maybe he had got the spade from work, or from his garage, or his neighbour's garage or from the garage of Samuel Baker, the guy, according to the licensing website, who owns the car he got into when he drove away. Maybe he had murdered Samuel Baker too. Or maybe Samuel Baker is the fat man.

I know so little but so much.

Seven

The police must be feeling as frustrated as me. There have been more stories in the newspaper, not that my mother has pointed them out. I wait until she goes to bed and then check front page to back, even the classifieds. Geoff Harris is dead, murdered, his body found in a burnt out car in a forestry block in the middle of nowhere. James Reed, known accomplice of Harris, 1.8m tall, approximately 130 kg, of European descent, long dark hair, brown eyes, beard, a picture included in the article, is missing. Both men have past convictions for growing and supplying cannabis (dope). Police want to hear from anyone who saw either of them prior to the night of the car fire or has seen James Reed since. Anyone who knows the whereabouts of James Reed should contact police immediately. James Reed should not be approached. James Reed is considered dangerous.

James Reed murdered Geoff Harris, even I can figure out that is what they think.

But James Reed didn't do it. He can't have. He was the fat man.

And now Geoff Harris is digging again for his money.

He waited a week before coming back, wanting a clear night and the moon to be completely full, I guess. I waited for him every night, just like I have waited a week for my parents to say something about the money that appeared in their mailbox, just like I have waited and watched for the red patch of skin on the back of my wrist to get better. None of them has happened, but now, on this cold night, Geoff Harris has come back. He digs slowly and carefully, methodically. This time he is digging to make sure the bag of money is gone – he is not digging to find it.

After he finishes each hole he carefully fills it back up, pushes the pine needles over the disturbed earth, marks the tree with a pocket knife and then goes to the next one. He has already fixed the mess he made a week ago. The area still looks as if it has been dug up, even through my night-vision goggles. But a nor'wester will bring down more pine needles, a possum will run through, maybe a snuffling pig, and soon you won't be able to tell at all.

The bandana is gone, and the dreadlocks. Geoff Harris has cut his hair, and shaved. And he's well dressed. No jeans with holes this time. It's still him, the same face, the same body, the way he moves, but he doesn't look like a dope grower anymore. He looks like a business man.

As far as I can make out, the same car he drove away in is parked on the gravel road. I think about circling behind him to have a closer look, maybe finding something that will tell me who this man really is, this man who burnt his own car with his friend's body inside, faked his own funeral, let his sister, who loves him, think he's dead. There could be a wallet, or a receipt or a piece of clothing on the passenger seat – some clue that I could follow up. But the night is too still, too quiet, the moon too bright for me to move. He could hear me, look up, and then I would be dead.

Like James Reed, the fat man.

I wonder how long he will dig holes for. I check my watch. It has been almost an hour since I found him, and he had done a lot before I got here. He started at the trees four rows in from the road, near the river stone, and is now seven rows in. He is digging on either side of where I had moved the stone marker, five trees either side. I said he was being methodical.

When he gives up will he leave quietly in his car and never come back? What else can he do? He can't go to the police and report that his bag with a million dollars inside it has gone missing, can he? Not when he's faked his own death. What had he planned to do with the money that he won't be able to do now? Was he going to buy a house or a fancy car, or go overseas? A million dollars isn't all that much money. You can't buy a farm with it without going to a bank, except maybe a very small farm.

Was a million dollars enough to kill someone for? Did he kill the fat man for the money or was there another reason?

There are too many questions and I can't think of a way to answer any of them. And I'm cold. Sitting here, still, has made me chilled. The frost is starting to settle, including on me. There shouldn't be any more frosts. It's spring. Geoff Harris is keeping nice and warm by shovelling. He even took his coat off before. I can smell his sweat. It's not fair.

He's stopped. I don't know why. Did he hear me move slightly, trying to get circulation back into my frozen feet? He's leaning on the spade handle, panting. Maybe he's not so strong and fit after all, but then he has dug an awful lot of holes. He kicks the pine needles back over the one he has just filled in and looks around, his eyes glancing right past the darkness that is me.

My morepork, who is sitting above me on a tree branch, fluffs up his feathers. He must be cold, too, from all this sitting and watching and waiting. Maybe that's what Geoff Harris is looking at, is hearing – my morepork. Geoff Harris shifts to another tree, still looking, peering into the forest. The round moon has given each tree its own spotlight but it's deceptive. There are more shadows than light. Two possums have been playing on my left for about ten minutes, circling up and down a narrow trunk chasing each other. Now they stop and watch the man carrying the spade. The possums, my morepork and me, all with our own night vision, watch as Geoff Harris, blinded by the dark and the moon, tries to see us. Tries to see if we are really there, or just imaginings.

The two possums jump from their tree and run into the darkness, scattering pine needles under their claws. Geoff Harris starts at the sudden noise and turns towards it, blundering to where he thought it came from.

'Who's there?' he calls out, cautiously.

The morepork answers with a flap of his wings and leaves me, probably to hunt. He can't spend all night watching this man dig his holes.

So now it is just me.

'Who's there?' he calls again. He grips the spade as if ready to swing it, to protect himself from whatever he thinks is out there.

I don't move. He's to my left, near where the possums were. There are about five trees separating us but it is darker here, in the forest, away from the road.

'I know you're there,' he yells into the blackness.

The possums don't bother to reply, if they are still around. They're probably long gone. My morepork will be catching moths.

'Show yourself.'

He is moving further into the forest. I need to turn around to watch him. He has gone right past me on my left and my neck is aching, but I don't dare move. Or shiver. I clench my teeth together to stop them chattering.

He edges back, still carrying the spade, hesitantly. From the forest, the possums grunt, a human-sounding grunt, and Geoff Harris' head whips up. I have to stifle a laugh. The possum duo, intent on their own games, won't even know they're messing with him.

He stares again into the darkness, searching, desperate, then drops to his knees.

'James, James is that you?' A sob comes from his throat.

I stiffen, ready to run.

'James? You know I didn't mean to. I didn't mean any of it to happen.'

He must think he's talking to the fat man, the fat man's ghost.

'I shouldn't have hit you but you made me so angry, and you went down so hard and you were dead. Just like that. I didn't mean to do it.'

He gets up off the ground, still staring at where the possums had been. Maybe there is a tree that looks like a person there, a shadow in the darkness, something.

'James, just show me where the money is. I need it; I need it to start fresh again, to set up business again.' He stares into the darkness. 'James?'

Finally, slowly, he seems to give up, stumbling through the pine needles where he has been digging and onto the road. He opens the boot of the car and throws the spade in and slams it shut. Geoff Harris stands on the road, taking one more look into the trees, but now, in the full glare of the moon, he won't be able to see a thing. No possums, no ghosts, no me. He lingers for a few moments then opens the car door and gets in. I don't bother to watch him drive off. I'm up and running back deep into the forest, trying to rid my body of the cold.

'You'll catch a chill, out there in the forestry.' I can hear my mother's voice from countless nights before this as she has clutched my frozen hands, kissed my blue nose when I have come inside. I have learnt how movement warms a body, even on the coldest night when the frost is settling or snow has fallen unexpectedly. Running through the trees I have my own personal heater inside me, keeping me warm and safe from my mother's lectures and threats to keep me confined to the house. Anyway, I have read that hypothermia is not a bad way to die. Most people don't even realise it's happening. They simply fall asleep. I could do that.

I think about Geoff Harris. I doubt he will come back again. He's talking to ghosts. Ghosts aren't real. I know that for certain. If anyone would have seen one, it's me. I spend all night awake, mostly in the dark outside and the half dark of my bedroom, and I've never seen a ghost, or heard one, whatever they are supposed to sound like. If the dead can come back and walk around us and talk to us then it is me they should be talking to. I'm the only one awake every night, all night.

Geoff Harris is stupid and is a scaredy cat. He doesn't even know the sound of one possum playing with another. He won't be back.

Eight

Farming, my dad says, is the only business that makes something out of nothing. By nothing he means the sun, which grows the grass, which the sheep eat, which makes them fat and their wool grow. No one has to buy sunshine. It's free.

If it wasn't for farming, if there were no sheep eating grass, there would be no tractor salesmen or fertiliser suppliers, no freezing works or wool scours, and then there would be no banks and no lawyers and no accountants, and then there's the supermarkets to feed all these people, and schools to teach the children, and the hairdressers to cut their hair. That is what our economy depends on – the sun, growing a single blade of grass for the sheep to eat. That's what he says.

Of course, he explained all this to me in the dark

one night, when we were shifting a mob of ewes.

Last night, I stuck a whole bundle of notes in an envelope and put it in the mailbox. Before I had only put in two thousand dollars. No one has still said anything about finding it. Maybe now they will, now that it's ten thousand dollars. I mean, surely finding ten thousand dollars in cash addressed to you in your mailbox should be some reason for celebration? I had typed the envelope up just as before with 'please use wisely' on it under my parents' names. 'Please use wisely' now sounds kind of weak but I have to stick with it, otherwise they won't think it's from the same person. If they thought lots of different people were putting cash in the mailbox they might get really worried.

So tonight, getting up, I feel excited. It's like being the tooth fairy and Santa Claus. I wonder what they will do with the money. I mean, I hope they use it to pay the interest owing on the farm but maybe there will be something left over. Maybe there will be enough left over for a new laptop for me.

I imagine my parents' conversation.

My dad: 'I've found another of those envelopes in the mailbox this morning.'

My mum: 'What envelopes?'

My dad: 'Ones addressed to us with 'please use wisely' on it. This one's got ten thousand dollars in it.'

My mum: 'Ten thousand dollars!'

My dad: 'What are we going to do with it?'

My mum: 'Well, it does say 'please use wisely'. Maybe we should use it to pay the bank.'

My dad: 'I wonder who could be sending us money like this.'

My mum: 'It could be lots of people. It's obviously someone who knows us, who knows we need it. It must be from friends.'

My dad: 'But why don't they just give it to us then, instead of like this, in an envelope?'

My mum: 'We wouldn't accept it, would we? We'd give it back, pretend we don't need it. Anyway, it doesn't matter who it is. Let's just do what they say.'

I wish I had been awake to hear it, to listen, smiling to myself. They won't guess it was me. They will never guess and I'm going to keep it a secret forever. I've worked out if I put ten thousand dollars in their mailbox every month the million dollars will last a hundred months, which is just over eight years. Which is a bit long. I probably will be dead by then. But if I give them more than that a month they might get worried, or not want to use it. Anyway, I can only fit ten thousand dollars in an envelope so that's what it's got to be.

Mum is heating up lamb stew, which they must have

had for lunch, otherwise it wouldn't be cold. Her viola case is open in the living room and there is music on the music stand. She is rushing cooking the stew, grabbing toast from the toaster before it pops, spreading it quickly with butter. The sun is still setting so she has the curtains drawn across the kitchen window. They're black-out curtains, the really thick type.

I wait for her to say something about the money.

'I have to go to Wellington next week,' she says, finally.

'Why?'

'The second violist has pneumonia. It's like the flu only worse. I have to go and play.'

'How long will you be gone?'

'Just over a week. I'll take the car and leave it at the airport on Saturday. First rehearsal starts at ten that morning and then the concert is on the following Saturday night. They've sent me the music.'

'I wish I could come with you.'

'Your father will need you here and, anyway, you have school work to do.'

'Nothing else been happening?' I try cautiously.

'No. Now eat your breakfast. I've got practice to do. Have you taken your vitamin pill?'

I listen to her play as I eat the stew and toast in the kitchen. It sounds like Bach. She stops a lot, and goes back to the start again and again. The piece is difficult. There are about twelve violists in the New Zealand Symphony Orchestra. There has to be so many because the viola is not very loud. There is only one tuba because it is really loud. There are more than twenty-five violinists divided into first violins and second violins – the first violins usually play the melody. The violas sit right in front of the conductor. To their right are the violins and to their left are the cellos and the double basses so all the strings sit at the front with the woodwind and the brass and the percussion instruments behind them. Orchestras have been organised like this just about forever. I follow what the symphony orchestra is doing by reading their website. They have their programme for the whole year on it, and information about all the musicians, including my mother. When she travels to Wellington to play, there is usually a special mention of her under *Latest News*.

I put my plate and fork and knife in the dishwasher and watch Mum from the doorway. She has her back to me. Her viola is tucked under her chin, her right arm has the bow and her body is bending and twisting with the music, like a tree in the wind. It is definitely Bach she is practising. I listen to the notes and wonder what it would sound like with a full orchestra playing with her. I could listen to the piece on the internet if I wanted, but it wouldn't be the same. My laptop doesn't have great speakers and really, I suspect, nothing could be the same as being there.

I'm turning away when I see it. On the mantelpiece, above the fireplace, is an old wooden clock. You have to wind it up. It's always showing the wrong time but for some reason Mum and Dad keep it going. Behind it, stuffed in the gap between its back and the wall are two envelopes. Both have been opened and I can just make out the hundred dollar bills inside them.

So, they did get the letters. They're just not saying anything about them. But they're keeping them.

A lot of people would probably worry about having that much cash in the house. It is only partly hidden behind the clock. I once said to my parents we should have a safe in the house to keep our valuables in, with a combination, even hidden behind a picture like in the movies. I've seen them advertised on the internet. They're not that expensive and our house is so far from anywhere. Someone could so easily walk in, steal everything. I mean, we never even lock the front door.

The next day, after they had laughed at me about the safe, Dad and I were doing the lambing beat in the back paddocks. It was early spring. He asked me how much I thought the flock was worth, just the ones in this paddock. I shook my head. I had no idea. He said they were worth more than anything we had in the house, and that anyone could drive up with a portable set of yards and a loading race and a sheep truck and steal the lot of them. Padlocks on gates, if we bothered with them, could be cut with bolt cutters. We can't put the sheep into a safe, so why should we worry about whatever we thought was valuable enough to steal in the house?

He said most people, most city people, just looked at a mob of sheep and saw nice white, woolly animals. Something for tourists to take photos of. But what they were really looking at was hundreds of thousands of dollars.

Tonight, Dad is in his office working on the computer. He sees me and jumps up to pull the curtains shut, even though it is almost dark outside. I get glimpses of a red sky, touches of gold.

'The tailing gang finished today,' he says.

'How did it go?'

'Yeah, good. Hasn't been the best of lambings, but it's what I suspected.' He doesn't take his eyes off the computer screen as he talks. 'Your mum told you she's going to Wellington next week.'

'Yes.'

'How about I take you out on the farm a few nights that week? The older ewes' lambs need to be tailed and there are a few other things you could help me with. About time we went possum shooting again.'

'Okay.'

'It won't interfere with your school work?'

'I'm all up to date.'

'Good.'

He lets me go.

In the forest, it doesn't look as though Geoff Harris has been back to dig any more holes, or to talk to any ghosts.

Nine

I often think about the way I would like to die.

I don't want to die in a hospital. I don't like hospitals. People fuss over you and then they leave you alone. All alone in that white bed with the sides up so you can't get out, with only a button to push if you 'need anything'. I've been in hospital twice, to have the start of skin cancers removed. The first time I can't remember because I was really little. The second time I was eight. Because the farm is so far away from the hospital my parents couldn't visit very much. They were busy on the farm. The other children there were nasty, or scared, or dying.

Every time my father visited he would bring a new toy, and it would break. He brought me a wind-up cat that I wound up so much it didn't walk and purr anymore. There was a remote control helicopter that crashed because I couldn't get the hang of the controls quickly enough, and there was a camera that some kid stole. My father would always apologise as if it was his fault and buy me another toy.

If this thing on the back of my wrist is a melanoma, then I will have to go into hospital to get it removed. Then there will be blood tests and scans to see if it has spread to my insides. If it has, there might be radiation therapy, which is when they put you under a light that burns the cancer, several times a week for months. More likely, there will be chemotherapy, which is drugs. It is either pills or they give it to you through a needle right into your vein. You have to sit in these big armchairs and wait for it to drip inside you slowly. As if the big chairs make a difference. Whichever way they give it to you, whether it's pills or through a needle, it makes you sick. You vomit lots. Your hair falls out. And I don't like needles that much.

One of the kids I email occasionally in the States had chemo two years ago. She told me about it.

It made me think about it all, about dying. I even started making a list – a list of the things I want to do before I die. I began to write it all down on a piece of paper, but I stopped and threw it in the fire just in case my mother found it. It had been my 'wild list', a list of impossible things like riding elephants across the Sahara desert, and swimming with hammerhead sharks in the Red Sea. But I also have (these are in my head) my 'emotional list' which includes falling in love and watching the sun rise and touch my skin and for it be okay. Then there is my 'practical list', which includes going to school – a real school, not correspondence school – and playing the viola in a youth orchestra.

Then I have a different list in my head of all the things that I *can* do, that I *do* do, that most kids never get the chance to. I know this is the most important list of all. On this list is riding a four-wheel motorbike, shooting a rabbit, looking at frost settle in the darkness, shearing a sheep, seeing comets and meteors and star showers and watching the Aurora Australis turn the night sky into giant wavering sheets of green and purple and every other colour. Most kids don't get to do any of that. Most adults don't either.

Once, I woke my parents to watch the aurora. I didn't know what it was. Well, I did, I had read about it on the internet, but I didn't know if this was actually it. Dad was really grumpy at getting woken up in the middle of the night, but Mum just stood there, in her dressing gown and slippers, watching. I liked that; I liked being able to share something of my world with them.

With my mother playing most evenings in the living

room, I've taken to practising in the woolshed. The nights are warmer now and I like the open space of the shearing board and the floor below, and my pretend listeners. I like how the shearing board creaks as I stand on it, as a real wooden stage might, and the corners of the shed are dark in the gloom, as a concert hall might be. I play Bach's *Concerto in C Minor*, the second movement, which is really slow and dreamy. I have played it so much I can almost do it from memory. Not that I try to memorise my music. There's no point is there? I'm never going to play in front of anyone who will be impressed that I can remember sheets and sheets of music.

I should have started the night's practice with scales and arpeggios but tonight I just want to play. An arpeggio is playing all the notes that make up a chord but one at a time. They're really boring. You go up and down, up and down. Etudes are more fun but real pieces are best. I have to tune the viola carefully to start with. The woolshed is cold compared with inside. The strings on the viola tighten or loosen with different air temperatures. They are slowly stretching all the time and after a bit they have to be replaced, but the coldness in the woolshed really upsets them. Inside, in the living room, I would use Mum's tuning fork but out here I just remember what the note

A sounds like and turn the peg for the top string until it sounds right and then tune the other strings, C, D and G, to it.

The Bach concerto is marked *Adagio molto espressivo*, which is Italian for 'slowly with lots of expression'. Bach was German, but everything in his music is written in Italian. I don't get that one. It's like he had to write in Italian to make his work look like real pieces of music. I mean this is Bach we're talking about. Anyway, I play slowly with much expression, not that there is any other way you can really do it.

I wonder what Dad is up to, what he is thinking. He doesn't play a musical instrument, or read music, or even really listen to it. Except, of course, when he's in the house and Mum or I are practising. He doesn't have much choice then. He listens to the radio in the ute and on the tractor, but it's always on one of the rock stations or easy listening or whatever. It's never on the classical programme.

It's strange, when you think about it, that Mum and Dad should be together as they have so little in common. It's amazing they even met. Dad grew up on a sheep farm not far from here. His parents were managers for a big corporate. They could never afford to buy their own farm. It was only after they died (a car accident – Dad doesn't talk about it) that their savings and the life insurance and what Mum had inherited from an elderly relation in England and what Dad had saved himself was enough money to buy a farm – this farm. And, really, it can't have been enough at all because now they have this huge mortgage.

Anyway, Mum grew up in Wellington and went to university there, studying the viola of course. She didn't know anything about farming, never thought about wanting to live on a farm. But one day Dad was passing outside a hall where she was performing and heard her play. He was in Wellington for some rugby game (he used to play rugby back then, just for his local club, not professionally or anything like that; he was an openside flanker) and he heard her and went in, even though he wasn't dressed right, and didn't know anything about the performance. He saw her play and, as they say, the rest is history. Mr Pearson and Mrs Pearson were married.

I like to hear Dad tell the story. He tells it better than Mum.

It was his idea to call me Viola – after the musical instrument that brought them together.

I continue to play slowly with much expression to the brooms and the wool bales and no doubt the rats. I hope they're all enjoying it.

When I'm finished, after about an hour, I take the

viola back to the house. The night is still, the stars out. I have time to go into the forestry.

As I lift the night-vision goggles out of their case by the back door, Mum finds me. She looks tired and is rubbing her left shoulder. I know she gets sore there when she practises a lot.

'I forgot to say earlier, I've got something to tell you.'

I stop what I am doing. Maybe this is it. Maybe she is finally going to tell me about the money in the envelopes, what they're going to do with it and how it will save the farm and everything. We won't have to leave.

'Well, what is it?' I say smiling, almost laughing out loud.

'A reporter rang today.'

'A reporter? What about?' My smile is gone. I'm worried. They haven't told anyone else about the money have they?

'Well, about you.'

'Me?' I relax. She must be joking around with me now.

'He's from the *Ashburton Guardian*. He wants to write an article about you.'

'What can they write about me?'

'About you having XP.'

'I hope you told them no. You did, didn't you?'

'No, of course I didn't. He's going to come tomorrow evening.'

'Mum, I don't want anything in the paper about me. I don't want people to read about me. How could you do this?'

I grab the night-vision goggles and run from the house.

'Viola, come back. Viola?' Mum calls after me but I don't stop.

Geoff Harris has not returned. There's just me and my morepork and the possums in the forest. And the trees. I sit down on the pine needles, lean back on a trunk and wait to see if he will come. There's a lot of pig sign about but I don't hear any pigs. Pigs root up the ground, make a mess. People occasionally come and hunt them with dogs as a sport and for their meat. The forestry people give out permits. I've never seen any hunters. Maybe people only hunt pigs during the day. The pig dogs sniff the pigs out and hold them until their owner gets there, following the sound of the squealing pig and of the dogs. Once, a hunter gave Dad a sow he had killed somewhere near here. It had a big knife hole in its neck and chest where he had stuck it and killed it. It was at least a hundred kilograms, far bigger than our biggest ram. Mum tried lots of different ways to cook the meat, but we were all glad when the last of it was gone, even though it was something different to the lamb we usually eat.

I think again about the fat man, how he died. I've read on the internet how a single punch can kill someone, if they fall wrong. The back of the head is soft; land on concrete or something hard with the back of your head and you are probably dead. Fat men would fall faster, harder. Geoff Harris is strong. He could land a pretty serious punch.

Maybe he panicked, so he bashed the fat man's teeth in so he couldn't be identified and burned the body in his own car. That way the police would think he had been murdered and the fat man was the one they had to catch. But they wouldn't be able to catch the fat man – they couldn't, could they? He was already dead.

I've read on the internet that the New Zealand Police get more than eight thousand reports of missing people every year. That's like a third of the population of Ashburton. Gone. So for the fat man to go missing is not unusual. It's the perfect murder. Not that any of it matters anyway. Two dope growers. One dead, the other missing. No great loss, as my father would say.

That pig sign is fresh, I'm sure of it. I didn't see it last night. Wild pigs, especially the boars – the male pigs – can be dangerous. They have tusks and can have a go at you. But worse still are the sows when they're protecting their piglets. Dad always says to keep away if I hear a pig. If one does try to attack me, he says I should yell at it as loudly as I can. Don't run. It will always be able to run faster. Yell and shout and scream and wave my arms at it, and maybe it might think twice and leave me alone.

Maybe sitting out here isn't such a good idea.

When I get back to the house, Mum is still up.

'I'm sorry about the reporter,' she tries.

I don't answer. Instead I pack the night-vision goggles into their case with more care than they need.

'He had seen some documentary on moon children somewhere and wondered if there were any in New Zealand, and he found out about you.'

I close the clasp carefully and put the case on the shelf.

'It would be good for people to know about you, understand the condition. It might help.'

'How will it help?' I ask, looking at her for the first time. She's wearing her dressing gown. The one she's had for, like, forever.

'I don't know but it might. People usually like to help, if you give them the chance.'

Ten

The reporter asks me lots of dumb questions. He comes after dark, so at least he's got that much intelligence, but it stops me going out into the forest. He takes up a whole hour of my time and asks things like, 'What does it *feel like* to be one of only a thousand people in the world to have this condition?' and 'Do you ever think about dying?' and 'What would you be doing right now if you didn't have XP?' (It's just after 11 pm by the time he asks me this – I would be in bed asleep of course, you idiot.) And then he starts making jokes about vampires and werewolves. Why does everyone do that?

Finally, he's finished. But then it gets worse. He's brought a photographer along with him. She wants a picture of me playing the viola and a picture of me with the night-vision goggles to go with the story in the paper. She mucks around with her camera a lot, and I don't make it easy for her. I don't like having my photo taken, even by my parents. My skin is so pale I look like a ghost, and then there are all the freckles and, really, let's face it, I look ugly. I look... I look as if I'm diseased.

Mum tells me off lots and apologises to the photographer and tries to get me to pose properly with the viola, and in the end I just do what I'm told. I'm over it. Let them do what they want to do. I don't care anymore.

When they finally leave, for the drive back to Ashburton, Mum is ready for bed so I can't go outside, not even to the woolshed. I stomp off to my bedroom and try to forget it all. I look over the sheet music of *Meditation* and play it in my head. I still can't get it right. I turn on my laptop and watch several versions of it that people have posted on YouTube, following the sheet music as it plays, watching each performer. They all perform with an accompanist on the piano. I've never played with an accompanist. We don't own a piano. I don't think we can afford one. Anyway, it wouldn't fit in our living room. Not a proper piano, a grand piano. I did ask Mum once. She can play the piano a little, but not well enough to accompany me.

She said it wasn't important, that I shouldn't worry about it. That practising on my own was fine.

Before I go to sleep, I look through the newspaper. A person has come forward. They saw Geoff Harris in the vicinity of the forest, hitching, the afternoon of the car fire. They had given him a lift into Ashburton. He had seemed agitated. Police want to know of any other sightings, especially of James Reed, of James Reed near the forest. Maybe they think he was waiting for Harris to return that day, waiting to kill him.

But he wasn't was he? Reed was probably already dead. Harris must have been seen dropping off the other car ready for that night's getaway.

My mother's playing enters my dreams as I wake the next evening. It is me who is holding the viola and the bow, me who is playing in the orchestra, watching the conductor and my place in the music, with the other musicians around me, the violins to my right, the cellos to my left, the oboes and the flutes behind, and right at the back of the stage I can feel the percussion booming. I don't want to open my eyes and find it all gone, hear only my mother's viola in the living room below me.

I eat the reheated chops and vegetables she has dished out for me and swallow my vitamin D capsule, drink the glass of milk. Tomorrow Mum is flying to

Wellington and there will be just Dad and me for the week, and I will have the living room back to practise in, if I want Dad listening.

She pauses, takes the viola out from under her chin and turns to me.

'Did you sleep well?'

'Yes. Is it okay if I go out to the forest?'

'Of course. I haven't got time to give you a lesson tonight, I'm sorry. One of the pieces we're playing, it's difficult.'

I rinse my plate and my glass and put them in the dishwasher.

Neither of us says anything about the reporter and the photographer. I get my jacket and head down the hallway towards the back door as Dad comes out of the office. He sits down in the living room. He only does that when he wants to talk to Mum. I stay silent and still by the door. They won't notice me, won't realise I'm listening, that I'm still there.

Mum puts the viola down, her words sharp.

'I'll bank it, if that's what you want.'

'We need this money,' Dad says, softly.

'You don't think I know that?'

'We'll lose the farm, we'll lose everything.'

'But we don't know where it came from.'

'Don't think about that, don't worry. Just be glad

that someone out there, for once, is giving us a hand. After all the bad things that have happened in our lives, let's just enjoy this one good thing. All right?'

'All right,' she replies, finally.

The next night, when I wake up, she's gone and so are the envelopes of money from behind the clock on the mantelpiece. I'm glad she's taken them. I know Dad was meaning me when he talked last night about the bad things that have happened to them both. At last I am becoming the good thing, even though they don't know it is me, will never know it is me.

The newspaper, open to the Saturday features section, is spread on the table, waiting. I look at the photo of myself playing the viola in the living room, and the smaller one of me holding the night-vision goggles, and turn away. I look horrible, abnormal. It's a freak show. The pictures take up the whole top half of the page, the story underneath. I fold the paper so I can't see myself, only the words. I don't want to read the article but everyone else in South Canterbury has by now, so I might as well too. Find out what everyone knows about me, find out what a hash job the reporter has made of it, of me dying.

There's several paragraphs about XP, and about how only a few people in the world have it. There's stuff about UV light, and the differences between sunlight and fluorescent lights and normal light bulbs, and then there's lots about me. About how I learn through correspondence school, how I help out on the farm, but only at night. About how I've never had the chance to go to a swimming pool, or play sport like other kids, or go to museums or art galleries or A&P Shows. There's a lot about my mother teaching me to play the viola. They must have interviewed her before I got up, or maybe the next day on the phone when I was sleeping. She says, in the story, that I'm gifted, that my musical ability is far beyond my years, that she has never come across a young person able to pick up pieces so easily and play them with such understanding. Someone who is so dedicated. She says that one day she would like to see me perform on stage in front of an audience.

I stop reading. I stare at the wall on the other side of the table, where the wallpaper has come away slightly at the join of the sheets and no one has ever bothered to glue it back down. I'm gifted. She wants me to perform. She has never told me any of this. I don't know whether to believe it or not. It takes so much work for me to get a piece of music right. Over and over I practise it and often I'm still not happy. I can't get it perfect, not always.

I started playing when I was seven. She wouldn't let me start before then, saying my hands were too little,

I couldn't reach all the strings, it would discourage me. Instead, I would sit on the sofa and listen and watch her play, and she would teach me the meanings of the funny looking squiggles on their five horizontal lines, what I know now to be bars of music and crotchets and quavers and minims. I could read music almost before I could read books. When I was really young I would sit on the sofa and wonder how something so beautiful could come from one person playing.

And then, when she finally handed me my own viola, I was so scared. It was a half-size one, my fingers would never have stretched to play one the size of my mum's, and she had bought it for me. I was terrified I wouldn't be able to play it; I wouldn't be able to transform the notes on the page to something beautiful the way she did. That first time I drew the bow across the strings, playing that first open note, my fingers gripped the instrument so tightly I was afraid I was going to break it. I wanted to shut my ears so I couldn't hear the horrible noise I would make. But the sound was beautiful. I could feel it resonating through the instrument and into my body. Before that, I never knew that happened. I never knew that the music came from inside you.

Eleven

I can still feel the warmth of the sun on the trunk of the pine tree, even though it is dark. When I told Dad I was going for a walk, he was struggling with the farm accounts. He won't stay up waiting for me. He thinks Mum is overly protective, that she shouldn't worry so much, that I'm tougher than she thinks. And he needs his sleep.

The night-vision goggles are slipping on my head so I have to stop and adjust the straps. There had been a lot in the newspaper article yesterday about them as well – how I go out at night into the forestry, about how the goggles work, about how they give me some freedom to be a kid, about what I get to see in the dark like the morepork I think of as my own, and the possums.

I wander over towards the forestry road where Geoff Harris left the river stone. There is nothing new. No sign of anyone. Just the two possums playing. I think they have made the area their home.

Possums have territories, just like most wild animals, and most people. The young males sometimes travel long distances, usually looking for a mate, but the females and family groups stay put. And they share nests, which isn't a good thing because that's how they give TB to each other. The science guys call it a 'hot spot'. A single male possum with TB will come and live in a new area and sleep in different nests and give it to all the other possums. But what's really amazing is how the TB is spread from the possums to the cattle on farms. The scientists used to think a possum with TB would cough its germs on the grass, then a cow would eat that grass and then get the disease. That was until they set up cameras in known hot spots. Possums are nocturnal, but when they are sick with TB they get disorientated and go out during the day. Cows are curious and want to know what the furry brown thing is in their paddock. They go and lick the sick possum, even throw it up into the air. They play with it, and that's how they get the disease. Sheep aren't curious. They just eat grass and know better. That's why sheep don't get TB. And everyone thinks sheep are dumb.

Interesting though, that people have to see things to believe them, to understand them. Don't draw conclusions until you have all the evidence I suppose.

I hope the two possums haven't got TB. They don't look sick.

In a few weeks I will put another ten thousand dollars in my parents' mailbox.

Maybe, with the money, my parents might do up the house a little, after they get the farm's mortgage down enough so the bank manager is happy. I haven't been in other people's houses; I haven't been in anyone's house except our own to compare, but I know ours is old. Everyone in those American TV comedies I watch has nice homes. They have fridges that make ice cubes and big sofas and shiny benchtops and bright coloured cushions. Our carpet is so worn in places you can't see the pattern anymore and in winter there is often ice on the inside of the wooden window frames. The doors of the kitchen cupboards always stick.

I'm not complaining; I like our house, but it would be nicer if it was warmer and brighter and more colourful. I think it would make my parents happier.

Geoff Harris, 37, of Ashburton, can't be living in Ashburton any longer, can he? Not if he's supposed to be dead. He's changed his appearance; he's no longer got the dreadlocks but even so, someone would still recognise him, if they knew him, bumped into him in the street by accident, and then it would all have been for nothing. He must have left the town, maybe left Canterbury, the South Island, New Zealand. New Zealand is only a small country. Mum is always coming back from her trips to Wellington with stories of how she bumped into this person or that person that she used to know years ago. Maybe that's why he hasn't been back to dig any more holes. He's left the country. Gone to live the new life he had planned. Maybe he had some other money stashed away that he's used, maybe hidden in another forest. He's dug that up and gone.

There is no one on the forestry road. I walk back to the house, my morepork flying from tree to tree above me. I practise *Meditation* in the woolshed until well after midnight, and I get it right. I get it perfect and it's beautiful and just the way Massenet, the brave soldier in the Franco-Prussian War who was too afraid to listen to his own music performed, would have wanted it. I imagine him, after I've played it in one of the great concert halls in Europe, desperately asking people from the audience as they leave, what was it like? Was it good enough?

'Bravo, bravissimo,' they would have said, and he would have smiled.

'Bravo, bravissimo,' the brooms and the bales of wool tell me from the woolshed floor and I bow to them, smiling.

Twelve

Traditionally in New Zealand, farming is a man's job. Women – the wives – help out. They are responsible for the house and the meals and the children. For making sure there is hot food on the table and clean clothes to wear. It's not sexist. It's just the way it is. To farm you have to drive tractors to use bale feeders or mowers or ploughs. You have to know how to fix them. You have to be able to build fences, use post drivers, strain up the wires, hang gates. You have to be able to move sheep or cattle around yards, draft them, drench them. You have to be brave.

I'm not saying that women can't do all these things, but it's just tough work, hard, physical work, out in the cold and the rain. If there was only Mum running the farm, she could get fencing gangs in to build the fences, there are contractors who will mow paddocks, spray gorse, but that costs more money than doing it yourself. And then there is always the stock work. A fully grown ram weighs more than 80 kg. If it wants to take you on, it will break your knee with one hit with its head, or if you are bending down to pick something up and don't see it, it will crack your skull open and kill you.

Because I'm a girl, it is unlikely I will inherit the farm – that is, if I even outlive Dad. Farms are handed down from father to son, in some cases for generations. That won't happen with this farm. If I live long enough, I could marry some nice young man who wants to go sheep farming, who Dad approves of, and together we could farm it, just like Mum and Dad have. But I will never have children, because they would be at least carriers of XP and I wouldn't do that. So even if this becomes a second generation farm, it will never be passed onto a third.

By being a girl, and by having XP, I break the New Zealand farming tradition that my parents had hoped, when they were young together, would be their future. Traditions are important. The world likes order and for things to stay the same. Like the trees in the forestry planted in straight lines. I am the ridge line, the hollow, the creek, which breaks the straight line. I am the bad thing that happened in my parents' lives.

We usually have about 400 old ewes in a separate mob that we lamb later than the rest of the flock. You can tell how old a sheep is by how worn its teeth are. Ones that are really old are called gummies. Old sheep don't get false teeth like old people do. Instead, they die of starvation because they can no longer chew the grass. Dad doesn't let that happen. He sends them to the works before that, or kills them for meat for the farm dogs. But first he tries to get one more lamb out of them, and, if they're in good enough condition, twins or maybe triplets. He lambs them later so there is more grass for them to eat, the weather is better. The drawn-out days and the sun makes the grass grow. He makes them lamb later by putting the rams with them later. Ewes are the females and rams are the males. The gestation period (how long they're pregnant) of a sheep is, on average, 147 days, so you just do the maths. The rams get the ewes in lamb, they get them pregnant. In other words, they have sex. Kids growing up on farms don't need to have sex education lessons. We just watch it happening.

The tailing gang finished the main flock last week. Tailing is a big job, so Dad always gets people in to help him, just like at shearing. But the old ewes he and I do together. He brings the mob down from the hills during the day and has them in the paddocks by the woolshed ready when I get up. The woolshed's big covered yards have lights and we do it in there. The tailing gang sets up their own portable yards in each paddock so the sheep don't have to be moved around, but there're no lights out in the paddocks and we have only one set of night-vision goggles, so Dad brings the sheep to the covered yards, instead of us going to them.

We use the huntaways at night. There are huntaway dogs and eye dogs. Huntaways bark and eye dogs just stare straight into the sheep's eyes. Sometimes it's like they're telling them what gateway to go through by using some sort of brain power, like dog-to-sheep telepathy. Anyway, it doesn't work so well at night, when the sheep can't see the dogs' eyes, so Dad always gets the huntaways out of the kennels and leaves the eye dogs to snooze. Tonight, the huntaways' barking easily pushes the ewes and their lambs into the yards from the paddock, even though they don't want to go in. The lambs get separated from their mothers in the confusion and the ewes turn back, standing up to the dogs, stamping their feet, calling for their lambs. The lambs don't sense the danger of the dogs, the instinct from the days when wolves hunted them in the wild isn't switched on in their tiny brains. Dad and I move in behind the dogs, shifting the stragglers, the confused, the scared.

'Viola! That one!' he's pointing at a lamb that has wandered away from the mob and is tottering towards me. I grab it, pick it up and tuck it under my arm. It doesn't protest, instead it almost snuggles into my body. Dad rushes at the last of the mob, one hand on the gate, the other holding a stick, and finally the sheep are in the yards. The dogs stop barking, sensing their job is, for now, done, but the noise from the ewes and lambs doesn't stop. It echoes against the corrugated-iron roof of the yards, the walls of the woolshed. I climb over the wooden railings and drop the lamb into a pen as Dad moves towards the drafting gate. The ewes have to be separated from the lambs. Already the dogs are in with the sheep, walking on their backs, moving them forward so they enter the narrow race where, as much as they try, they can't turn around and go back. They have to go towards the gate that Dad is moving as if it's second nature for him – ewes go to one pen, lambs to another. It has to be done as quickly as possible or the lambs can smother in the crush of animals.

Dad only stops when there is space in the first pen. He lets the ewes he has drafted back out into the paddock. Some of them drift away, their heads down eating the grass, but the rest stay by the yards patiently waiting for their lambs. These are old ewes. They know what is going to happen. They have done it many times before.

By the pen where the lambs have been drafted into, where I had dropped the lamb, Dad has already set up the tailing chute and has the iron heating. It uses gas and the smell of gas and burnt flesh always hangs around the covered yards for days afterwards. I'm in the pen with the lambs. They stand on my feet or butt their heads against the rails trying to escape, or they stop still and bleat for their mothers. Some of them are really young, only three weeks old, but most are more like five weeks. They have Texel dads, which is a meat breed, so they will all be big and heavy, even the young ones, to pick up. And they will all go to the works when they are up to weight after Christmas. We use Texels as terminal sires. None of these lambs will be kept to become mums one day in the flock so none of them will be ear marked to show that they are ours. Terminal means terminal.

Dad is ready for me on the other side of the pen and I pick up the lamb closest to my feet and slide it, bum first, into the tailing chute. Before I let it go I inject it into the neck quickly, pushing the needle through the skin and into the muscle and pressing the plunger down all the way. The injection is a vaccination against things like tetanus. I have the bag of vaccine on a cord around my neck and it refills the syringe straight away ready for the next lamb.

Meanwhile, Dad is scratching the inside of its back leg with the scabby mouth vaccine (sheep can gets lots of diseases) then he grabs the tailing iron and cuts the lamb's tail off. The hot iron stops any bleeding. The lamb cries out and then it falls from the chute and down by Dad's feet. By that time I already have another lamb ready for him.

When I first watched tailing (I was too young to help), I thought it was awful and cruel and a horrible way to treat baby lambs. Dad said nothing, didn't explain why we did it or anything. Later on that summer we found a lamb that had missed the muster, that had not been tailed. Its tail was stuck down to its back legs with its own shit but that wasn't what was horrible. Flies had laid their eggs on the mess and the eggs had hatched out and the maggots had eaten through the lamb's skin and into the leg muscles. It was being eaten alive.

Dad picked the lamb up, it was too sick to run away, and brought it back to the woolshed on the motorbike and carefully crutched it (that is, shore the wool and the dags off its bum) under the lights on the shearing board. Blood oozed out of the open wounds. Then he poured on a white liquid and the maggots started coming out of the raw flesh, big fat white wriggling maggots. The liquid was killing them and any eggs left. It was foul. It was the worst thing I have ever seen. I almost puked watching it. The lamb lived but Dad said if we hadn't found it that night it wouldn't have made it. It would have been dead by morning.

After that I understood why we tail the lambs.

The last few in the pen are the hardest to catch. I always try to corner them. The dogs want to help. Jim jumps in with me until Dad yells at him to get out. He gives me a forlorn 'well, I tried to help' look before he obeys. He's too hard on the lambs and he knows it. I finally lift the last one into the tailing chute, inject it and then we are ready to draft again. Dad lets the lambs that have been tailed into the paddock and the mothering back up starts. The lambs, in pain and confused, bleat out for their mothers and the ewes rush up when they hear them call. I've never worked out completely how they do it. Some of it is the sound they make, each one must have its own distinct call even though I can't pick the differences, and then they sniff each other. When there is recognition the lamb instantly feeds from the mother, butting its head against her udder to let the milk down, then the ewe leads it away from the noise and the others to a quiet place in the paddock.

We draft again, fill the pens up, make sure they are not too full, and start tailing.

The boy lambs get extra attention – a rubber ring around their balls, their nuts, which will make them into wethers and not rams. The meat from rams is not very nice. It's tainted, it smells. That's why we make them into wethers. When the boy lambs are put back on the ground afterwards they sit down straightaway. That rubber ring on their nuts must really hurt. Sometimes it's good to be a girl.

Dad and I don't talk much when we work together. Just enough to get the job done. I might ask a question if I don't understand something, he might tell me something when he sees I've forgotten it but otherwise that's it. It's just the way we are together.

When we've finished, it's past midnight. Dad turns off the gas to the tailing iron and then flicks the switch that turns off the lights in the covered yards. I pick up my night-vision goggles from where I had left them on the steps to the woolshed and pull them on to my head.

'I'll just go put the dogs away,' Dad calls. 'You go back to the house and put the jug on.'

'Okay.'

I walk to the house. My arms and back are aching from picking up so many lambs, my hands can still feel pushing the needle through the skin of each lamb's neck. I stretch out my shoulders and look around at the stars and the trees in their shades of green and grey and white through the goggles. There, on the edge of the forestry, is someone. He's standing. Not moving at all, watching.

Geoff Harris is watching me.

Thirteen

Dad has left the back door light on. There is no way of turning it off except from inside the house. I can hear him start to shut the dogs in their kennels. Jim, my dog, has come to find me. He's stepped into the light. He wants a last pat, acknowledgement from me for a night's work well done. He doesn't sense the danger.

'Jim,' Dad shouts from the kennels. 'What a go, Jim.'

Jim, his white chest and golden coat glowing in the light, looks up at me, then he comes forward, pushing his nose into my trembling hand. I give him a pat.

'Go,' I tell him and he's gone.

Geoff Harris is still standing there. It's not dark, not totally dark. There're stars and a bit of a moon. In the light from the back door he can see me. He would have seen me and Jim.

'What are you doing standing out here?' Dad calls to me. 'I thought I told you to go put the jug on.' He is walking towards the house, torch in hand, the beam wavering on the ground in front of him.

'Dad?'

'What's up?'

Geoff Harris is gone. He was standing there, in the trees looking at me, and now's he's not.

'Nothing.'

'You seeing ghosts or something out there with those goggles?'

'I thought I saw something. It's gone, whatever it was.'

Dad swings the torch beam over towards the forestry, but there are only trees and darkness.

'Let's get you inside. It's cold,' he says, opening the back door, taking off his gumboots. Inside, I shakily put the night-vision goggles away in their case as Dad finishes washing his hands in the tub. When he has gone, I turn back to the door and lock it, pushing the little lever down so the snib catches in its groove.

I wash my hands, too, trying to get the smell of sheep off them. Then I pad quietly to the front door in my socks and lock it as well. Dad already has a cup of tea waiting for me in the kitchen. Mum always makes me a hot chocolate, but Dad drinks tea so that's what he makes me as well. We sit at the kitchen table not talking, sipping the hot drinks. If he senses I'm scared he doesn't say anything. Scared people are meant to look pale. Maybe he doesn't notice because I'm always pale. He finds a packet of supermarket biscuits in the pantry. Mum must have been so busy practising she didn't have time to bake before she left. We crunch on the biscuits, the unfamiliar taste.

'Well, I'm going to bed,' Dad finally says and gets up. He puts his empty cup in the dishwasher. 'Make sure you have a shower.'

'I will. Goodnight, Dad.' The shower thing is not about treating me as a little kid, it's about reminding me of the diseases and the skin infections you can get from handling the sheep.

I hear him in the bathroom upstairs, the shower running already. He won't take long. Two minutes if that. Dad is not one to stay in the shower for ages standing under the hot water. He says that's a girl thing, accusing Mum and me in the one go.

I turn all the lights off in the kitchen and move around in the darkness by feel. I pull back one of the living-room curtains, just enough so I can see the edge of the forestry. Without the night-vision goggles I can't tell if he is still out there or not, if he's still watching.

I quietly check all the doors and all the windows are locked before going upstairs.

My shower is quick. I've watched the Hitchcock movie *Psycho* on the internet. The shower scene is pretty gruesome, when the woman gets it through the shower curtain, although I have read they used chocolate sauce as fake blood (it's a black-and-white movie), which makes it a lot less frightening when you know that. Even so, as I said, I have a quick shower.

I turn on my laptop as I get dressed again, still thinking about Hitchcock and all his movies. I've watched a lot of them. I don't really read books. I mean, why would you, if you can watch the movie? Mum used to get books out of the library for me, she'd order them and they would arrive in the mail, but I just don't read. I have the internet. And that's what I turn to now. I google Geoff Harris again. There's nothing, nothing of any use. I even think of trying to somehow hack into the police computer files, but I haven't got a clue how to do it. In the movies it looks so easy. I google how to be a hacker and then get worried about googling things like that in case it throws up a flag somewhere, an alert, and my internet access gets shut down. Instead I try other search engines; I look at newspaper sites; I search everywhere and everything I can think of but there is nothing that could be about my Geoff Harris.

What I do find is my story, on the *Ashburton Guardian* website. I look at the photo of me with the night-vision goggles and then it clicks, everything slides into place. Geoff Harris must have read the article in the newspaper on Saturday. He's figured it out, that I live next to the forestry where he buried the money, that I have night-vision goggles, that I was watching him when he dug the hole.

But if he no longer lives in Ashburton, how would he have read the local newspaper?

He must have read it online. I thought the paper's website only had the front-page news, not the Saturday features. I should have checked. I should have known. He's been searching the internet, just like I have been to find him, to find me.

Has he guessed that I have his money?

I don't go to sleep until dawn, when I hear Dad up and moving around downstairs.

For breakfast, I cook myself sausages and eggs and swallow my vitamin D pill. It's help yourself when Mum's not here. Dad is on the computer in his office, so the living room is free. I lock all the doors and windows, then pull out my music book and find the next piece my mother wants me to learn to play. It's by someone called Marais. I get my laptop from my bedroom and google him. He's a French composer. Marin Marais lived from 1656 to 1728 and played in the royal court at Versailles near Paris. There's a painting of him wearing a long, powdered wig, tights up past his knees, and one of those gowns with big puffy sleeves. The French Revolution was 1789, so he missed all that, otherwise I think he would have probably been a contender for the guillotine.

La Provençale is from *Five Old French Dances for viola (or violin or violoncello) with pianoforte accompaniment.*

The first notes sound awful. Mum really wants me to play this? I try them again. The music has *gai* written above it, which means it's meant to be played cheerfully. Maybe that's the problem. I don't feel exactly cheerful. I slowly go through the piece but it doesn't get any better. Maybe the French Revolution should have happened a bit earlier.

'What is that?' Dad has put his head round the door.

'Sorry, it's what Mum wants me to practise next. I don't like it either.'

'Play that other thing, the one you were practising last week. That was better.'

I fumble through the sheet music and find Massenet's *Meditation*. Dad has never asked me to play for him before. He is sitting on the sofa, leaning back into the cushions, waiting. I place the viola under my chin and begin.

When I have finished he's silent for a moment, 'I've always loved that piece. You know what it's about?'

I shake my head.

'It's from an opera. An Egyptian courtesan, that's like a princess, chooses the love of God instead of the love of a man. Your mother used to play it a lot. She told me about it. But it's not really about all that, you know, religion and stuff, it's about making choices. About making choices and sticking with them. Accepting them. So, you're not going out into the forestry tonight?'

'No.' I draw my eyes away from the faded carpet and look at the sheet music again.

'Tomorrow night, how about we go spotlighting? See if we can find a few possums?'

'Okay.'

'Hey, when I got up this morning, all the doors were locked. Was that you?'

'Yeah, just with Mum away, you know.'

'Whatever, it doesn't matter. Another few days and she'll be back.'

The next night, when I get up, Dad tells me Jim has died. He had found him in his kennel that morning. He was an old dog. Old dogs die. He's already buried him.

And it's raining outside, so maybe tomorrow night for spotlighting?

And he's already locked all the doors.

I nod into my meat pie (two minutes in the microwave from the freezer, a couple more minutes under the grill to crisp up the pastry).

I practice *La Provençale* in the living room, over and over. It's boring. It's crap. I hate it. And my dog's died and I'm playing a gay piece of music that no one will ever hear me play except my dad and my mum when she finally comes home but that doesn't matter anyway because the sore on my wrist is getting worse. It must be a melanoma. Melanomas grow beneath the skin. Already I can feel its tentacles reaching inside me to my lungs and liver and my brain. Jim and I will be dead together, buried deep as the rain seeps into the ground above us.

Fourteen

The moon and the stars are out tonight. The rain cleared in the morning, Dad said. We're bouncing around on the four-wheel motorbike in the paddocks looking for possums, or rabbits, or anything else to shoot. I've got the night-vision goggles on and am holding the gun while Dad drives. The bike headlights bounce along with us on the ground. One of my hands is wrapped tightly around the back of the bike frame and the other is just as tightly hanging onto the gun. I search a tree break but see nothing. If I had, I would have stopped Dad by yelling in his ear, or letting go of the bike frame and tapping him on the shoulder, but I don't so he keeps driving.

I checked the edge of the forestry when we left the house. There was no sign of Geoff Harris, no sign of anyone watching the house, watching for me.

Neither Dad nor I are wearing motorbike helmets. I was reading the other day, in one of the farming newspapers, that the government is having a crackdown on four-wheel motorbike riding on farms. There have been too many accidents, too many deaths, so it's no passengers, no kids riding them and everyone must wear a helmet. Inspectors are walking on to properties, without ringing up first, to check if farmers are obeying the rules and, if they're not, they're giving them tickets. Big fines. It seems wrong to me. I mean, I can drive Dad's ute around the paddock and that's not illegal even though I don't have a driver's licence, am too young to have one, but these people can walk on to our place and have a go at us about how we ride a motorbike? Anyway, Dad doesn't seem too worried about it. Maybe the inspectors don't come out at night. Maybe they're too afraid of vampires and werewolves.

We're breaking all the rules. No helmets, me a kid and a passenger and holding a gun. I'm sitting on the side of the bike, with both of my legs together behind one of Dad's. It means he has to balance the weight of the bike by leaning more to the other side but it works. When we shift stock at night, Jim usually sat on the other side of the back of the bike with the rest of the dogs running behind us. Top dog, old dog, got the easy ride, my fingers entwined in his long coat. Except, that won't happen anymore.

Dad stops the motorbike and reaches around for the gun.

'Possum, in the tree over there,' he says. He must have caught the glint of its eyes in the motorbike headlights.

I pass him the gun and hop off the bike, give him room to shoot. I can see the possum now. It stares at us unmoving, trapped in the light. Its fluffy tail is wrapped around the branch it's sitting on. Dad shoots and it falls to the ground. It is pretty rare that he misses, unless I've knocked the gun's sights or something. We both run forward to pick it up. Sometimes they're still alive and that can be pretty scary. They're all teeth and claws and ready to fight, but this one is dead. I kick it just to make sure then pick it up by its tail, carry it back to the bike. It's a big male. Sometimes the females have joeys in their pouches. Possums are marsupials, just like kangaroos.

We ride around for another hour but don't see anything else except a couple of hares, which are gone before Dad can even reach for the gun. Giving up, he lines up a few targets for me – the knot in the wood of a fence post, a small stone on top of an outcrop. There's nothing behind them if I miss. A bullet from a twenty-two can travel two kilometres. But I don't miss. I am my father's daughter.

Back at the house, Dad throws the dead possum into one of the dog kennels. Dogs get fat eating possums, he says. The dog, Jan, an eye dog, wakes up and comes out to sniff the still-warm body but then goes back inside her box. Beside her kennel, Jim's is silent and empty.

I scan the edge of the forestry but there is no one there, no one watching us.

The rest of the night I spend doing school work. Somehow, I've got behind.

I'm practising *La Provençale* in the living room the next evening when Dad comes in.

'Don't you go out walking in the forestry anymore?' he asks.

'I just want to get the piece figured out before Mum gets home.'

'I'd go for a walk if I was you. The stars are out. And that thing you're playing still sounds awful.'

'Maybe later. Does it sound that bad?'

'It's not your playing; it's the music.'

He leaves me to it. I struggle through *La Provençale* again, thinking about the forest, thinking about Geoff Harris.

Later, after Dad has gone to bed, I turn out all the lights and put on the night-vision goggles. I quietly open the back door. It swings silently on its hinges and I tread softly down the concrete steps, closing the door behind me without a sound.

I look over at the edge of the forestry. There's no one there. I move around the side of the house and again look for any sign and there is nothing. I am alone.

Maybe he came to look that night, after reading about me in the paper, and decided it wasn't worth it. Maybe he took pity on me, understood my situation, that it's worse than his, that we need the money more. Maybe he realised that since I have kept my mouth shut so far, I'm not going to blab now.

Still, I don't venture into the forestry. Instead, I go into the woolshed and remove the boards from the shearing stand floor and take another ten thousand from the bag, even though the month is not up. I stuff the money into my jacket pocket and zip it up closed. On the way back to the house, I check the edge of the forestry again, but I don't see anything.

The next night Dad doesn't talk to me. Not about the money anyway. He's found it. The opened envelope is stuffed behind the clock on the mantelpiece just like the others had been. I don't say anything and he doesn't say anything. He stays in the office. Maybe he is counting the envelopes in the top drawer of the desk, wondering who's been using so many. I practise *La*

Provençale and get it as good as I'm ever going to get it. Mum is back tomorrow. I will be ready for her with it. Her gifted child. Then I play *Meditation*, just to see if Dad will come into the room to listen and talk. But he doesn't. Maybe some tax return or something is due.

When he says goodnight, I pack away my viola and put on the night-vision goggles.

The stars are out. The wind that shook the house earlier in the day, waking me from sleep at least twice, has left. There is just me outside. It's quiet and still and seems safe, even though my heart is beating so hard I feel it's going to burst out of my chest. I have wavered all evening, since I got up, about whether to walk in the forest tonight or not, but now I know, as I touch the first pine tree trunk and feel its rough bark, the sticky sap, that it's okay. It is good to be back after what seems such a long time away.

I wander through the trees and catch up with the possums, but they ignore me, as usual, too intent on their own games. The wind has brushed the floor of the forest, under the trees where Geoff Harris and I dug for the money. The pine needles are neat and tidy once more. It's as if nothing ever happened here. Even the river stone is gone. Maybe Geoff Harris took it with him that last night he was here, when he watched me, when he realised there was now nothing he could do.

Suddenly I feel free and empty and happy. It's over.

The stars shine through the slivers of sky that the trees shape as I dance through their open corridors. The air is changing, is charged. A storm is brewing on the other side of the mountains, to the west. The Southern Alps usually shelter us from the rain, but often we still get the lightning and the thunder. It is spectacular to watch in the dark. I hurry to the edge of the forest, towards home, so I can see the skyline, but the first crack of thunder explodes well before I get there, and another. Then it's full on.

My feet slip on the pine needles but I laugh, running even faster through the trees, my hands reaching out to their trunks as I pass each one.

At the forest's edge, I linger, looking at the house. Everything is dark. The storm is stirring the tree tops. This was where Geoff Harris stood, that night we tailed the lambs, when he watched me. I look around by my feet but there is no sign that he was ever here. No empty Coke can or food wrapper, no disturbed ground. Maybe I imagined it. Maybe it was just a trick of the light made by night-vision technology. Maybe I have been so scared, so petrified, for nothing.

Lightning flashes above the mountains, white against white, their still-snowy peaks bright through the goggles, and then the thunder rolls down the ridges to me. I watch in awe at the power of the storm and the strength of the mountains blocking it, preventing it from leaving the west.

There is a noise above me, a soft thud repeated with each gust of wind. At last I take my eyes off the mountains and look up.

It's my morepork.

He's hanging, a piece of rope around his neck, swinging in the wind, hitting the trunk of the tree, making the noise.

When I reach him, struggling up through the lower branches, he is still warm to touch. The blood from the holes the shotgun pellets have made is wet against my fingers. The rope has been tied as if it's a hangman's, the rope coiled around itself in a slip knot, even though my morepork was already dead when the noose was put around its neck. The sound of the thunder must have covered up the shotgun blast.

I hurriedly untie the rope from the branch and run to the woolshed where the shovel is. There is a rambling rose by the woolshed door. That is where I bury my morepork. I'm too afraid to go back into the forest to bury him where he belongs.

Fifteen

'I didn't want you to play that.' Mum is tired from travelling all day and now exasperated with me. I have slept late and she wanted to talk. I have made her wait.

I slept late because I didn't fall asleep until well after dawn, until well after I heard Dad get up and cook his breakfast and unlock the doors to the house and go off on the motorbike, the dogs barking. I had locked them again as soon as he was gone, dressed in a coat and gloves and hat so the sun from the windows didn't get on my skin. During the night I had connected the death of my morepork with the death of Jim. I understand the message now, the message from Geoff Harris, that I hadn't understood when Dad had told me my dog was dead. That I or my parents, or all of us, will be next. He saw me, under the back door light, patting

Jim. The golden dog that looked nothing like any of our other dogs. He would have found him easily in the line of kennels. He saw my morepork when he was digging the holes, looking for his money and it was in the *Ashburton Guardian* story, how I had got to know the animals and the birds that only come out at night, like me.

Geoff Harris wants his money back and he is telling me by starting to kill the things that I care about. I have read about people like him on the internet. They start with animals, like people's pets, and then they kill the owners.

I play *La Provençale* for Mum. Dad is sitting next to her on the sofa grimacing the whole way through.

'Marais is a terrible composer,' she continues. 'I mean, he was good in his day but what has come since him is so much better.'

'It was the next piece in the book. I thought you wanted me to learn it.'

'I was going to get you to skip it. I was going to play it for you, so you knew it and understood it, but I never expected you to learn it.'

'Play the other one, play *Meditation*,' Dad says to me. 'It's good,' he tells her.

I shuffle through the pages and find the music, put the viola under my chin again. I play it, but even from the opening bars I know I'm not playing it for my mum, or my dad. I play it for Jim and my dead morepork and the choices I will soon have to make even though I don't know what they are. What I can do? How I can keep us all safe? When the last notes die away I pack my viola back into its case. I can't play anymore.

'That was beautiful,' Mum says finally.

'Told you,' Dad says to both of us.

It is the first praise she has ever really given me but somehow it doesn't matter now. Not a lot matters.

'I thought I'd go for a walk,' I say.

'Of course, just, before you go, I've something to tell you,' Mum says.

I look up at her. She's got off the sofa, is excited about something.

'You know the story in the *Ashburton Guardian*?'

I nod.

'Well, the response to it has been amazing. They want to open the city up for you at night. The swimming pool and the art gallery and the museum. Even McDonalds. I suppose we can go there. They'll have to turn off all their fluorescent lights. They never knew about you. They want to help. They even want you to play, in a concert, especially for you.'

'But I can't swim. I don't even have a bathing suit.'

I run out of the house, grabbing my jacket and the

night-vision goggles on the way. I slam the back door. I don't mean to, but I do.

In the woolshed I stand on an empty bucket, my fingers frantically feeling in the dust for the key to dad's gun cabinet. By law, all guns have to be locked up in New Zealand. The police inspect the gun cabinets when they renew the gun licences every so often. The bullets are meant to be in a different place, but Dad doesn't bother with that. And the key is supposed to be hidden elsewhere as well. Dad just keeps it on top of the cabinet.

Inside are Dad's shotgun, the twenty-two, and the three-oh-eight, which is big gun, for taking out something like a deer or a cattle beast. I use the same key to unlock the padlock on the old fishing tackle box that sits on the top shelf of the gun cabinet. I take out the magazine of bullets for the twenty-two. I check that it is full, slip it into the slot in the gun and take off the safety catch.

Outside, the lights are on in my parents' bedroom. Dad must be going to bed. The living room lights are also on, so Mum must still be up. I skirt the house and slip out the back gate, towards the forestry. There's a place, a tree by itself, where I can sit and watch the house and the forest and the woolshed and anyone who might be moving in between. The darkness of the trunk will hide me from anyone looking. I scoot over to it, the gun ready in my hands, just in case.

The trunk of the tree is hard against my back, the ground cold under my legs. I keep the twenty-two tucked in next to me, in case someone is looking, but I can't see anyone. Yet. When I do they're going to get it.

My mind wanders, even though I'm trying to focus on the forest and the space between it and the house and the farm buildings. I think about what Mum said, about people wanting me to do things in Ashburton, about swimming. I don't have a bathing suit because I don't swim, have never had the chance to learn to swim, and I don't want one. I don't want people to see my body, how white it is, how undeveloped it is. I mean, I'm fourteen and I still don't wear a bra. I've got nothing. It's like puberty has forgotten me. It's saying I'm going to die anyway so why even bother getting periods and breasts and all of that. You're never going to fall in love, you're never going to have babies. Mum gave me the big talk a couple of years ago, about what would happen and I shouldn't worry about it and it was natural. I mean, I knew it all, she didn't have to tell me. I watch *South Park* on the internet, I know stuff, but knowing it doesn't mean your body is going to do it.

I'm not wearing a bathing suit. I don't care. That's it.

If there had never been that article in the newspaper then none of this would be happening. Geoff Harris wouldn't know about me and no one would want me to go swimming.

And Jim would still be alive. And my morepork.

The lights in the living room have gone out. Mum, probably still angry with me, must have decided not to wait up. She has gone to bed.

I shuffle against the tree trunk, trying to get more comfortable. It's too warm for a frost but it's still cold. I watch for another hour, the stars slowly wheeling above me. It's late, nothing is going to happen tonight.

Geoff Harris can send me messages by killing Jim, by killing my morepork, but I can send him messages too. I get up and run back to the woolshed. I lock away the magazine in the fishing tackle box, and the twenty-two next to the shotgun, just like they were before. In the house, in the laundry by the back door, is a box of my old toys. I don't know why Mum has kept them, but there is a toy car. I pad into the kitchen in my socks and find a piece of paper and a red pen. I draw lots of flames and cut them out with the scissors from the drawer and then stick them to the car with sellotape. And I grab some string.

Back outside, with the night-vision goggles on, I run to where my morepork was left dead, and reach up to the highest branch that I can. When I'm finished I look at my message to Geoff Harris. Hanging in the tree is the toy car with its paper flames. He will realise, when he sees it, that not only do I have his money but I also know he set the car on fire, he killed the fat man and burnt his body – that he better leave me and my family alone, or I will tell.

Back inside, I lock all the doors and make sure the windows are fastened shut.

Sixteen

Mum has bought me a bathing suit from a clothing mail order catalogue. It's green. She has bought three different sizes and will send the two back that don't fit for a credit. She expects me to try them on.

I take them upstairs to my room, close the door, sit on the bed and do nothing. I don't even look at them.

'Viola, which one fits?' she calls up the stairs to me.

She knows I'm not trying them on. She would be able to hear me moving around if I was trying them on and I'm not. I'm silent. I'm still.

'Viola?'

'I'm putting them on, all right?' I yell at her through the closed door.

I hear her sigh and walk back into the living room. Then next minute I hear her playing Bach or Brahms or something. The concert in Wellington had gone well. The first viola player or the conductor or someone wants her to be with the orchestra full time. She's thinking about it.

As I listen to the music I reach across and feel the bathing suits. The fabric is soft and stretchy. I slip off my jeans and my T-shirt and everything else so I'm naked then pull the smallest size on. It fits. There is no mirror in my room – I don't like to look at myself – but I can feel it fits, feel it covering what it needs to cover, and it's not saggy anywhere. It feels good on, like a second skin. I don't want to take it off.

Downstairs, I hand Mum back the bathing suits.

'The smallest one,' I tell her.

'The smallest one?'

I don't answer. What did she expect? Does she never look at me, never realise just how little and undeveloped I am? Maybe she doesn't like looking at me, just like I don't. I don't blame her.

I go into the kitchen and get rid of my half-eaten breakfast down the kitchen waste unit and put the plate and knife and fork in the dishwasher. I wasn't hungry anyway. I haven't been hungry for days. Maybe it is the cancer spreading in my body, the strands from the tumour on my arm wrapping themselves around my stomach. Maybe, one day soon, I won't be able to eat at all.

'Are you going into the forestry tonight?' Mum asks from the living room.

'No.'

'I didn't realise, until I heard what you told that reporter, how much you knew about the animals, about moreporks.'

I wipe down the kitchen bench, clean up the toast crumbs.

'You should go out. It's a nice evening. It's almost summer. You won't get the chance tomorrow night. We're going into Ashburton. You haven't forgotten have you?'

'No.'

'We've got to leave not later than 8.15. They're meeting us at the museum at 9.30 then there's the art gallery and McDonalds.'

'If you didn't want me to learn to play that French composer, who did you want me to play?'

'*La Provençale*? It was okay that you learnt it, don't get me wrong.'

I've come out of the kitchen, leaning against the living room doorway.

'I just wanted you to learn something more modern. I wanted you to learn the Vaughan Williams piece.'

'Who's Williams?'

'Ralph Vaughan Williams, he was a British composer. He only died in the 1950s, not hundreds and hundreds of years ago like Marais. And he was a great teacher and did so much for musicians and orchestras. He influenced so many other people to write music.'

'Is that what you want me to do now? Write my own music?'

'You can do whatever you want.'

I stand there, staring at her, with her staring back. There is a precipice between us. She's waiting for me to say the wrong thing, to jump off the edge, to tell her what I think. And she knows it won't be nice; it won't be pleasant. And then she will say what she thinks, and then I will stomp from the room, yell, cry, slam doors. She's daring me to do it, daring me.

There's a knock on the door.

It is such an unheard sound in this house. Hardly anyone comes here and the few who do, the bank manager, my correspondence school teacher, are always expected.

Dad comes into the room.

'Was anyone meant to be visiting tonight?' he asks.

'No, not that I know of,' Mum says.

'I'll go and see who's there,' Dad says, and walks down the hall.

Mum instantly begins to tidy up the unfolded newspaper on the coffee table and rearranges the cushions on the sofa. I think about how fast I can run

133

to Dad's gun cabinet in the woolshed. While Mum plumps up cushions, I wait for Dad to open the door and see Geoff Harris standing there, and the noise of the shotgun blast that will follow.

Instead there's quiet conversation and feet coming towards us.

'It's the police,' Dad tells Mum, who is now waiting in the living room doorway. 'They want to talk to Viola.'

'To Viola? Why?'

I'm standing right there and they're ignoring me.

Two men walk into the room and instantly it seems to shrink. They don't look like cops. They're both wearing jerseys, shirts with ties and dark pants.

'Detectives Shaw and Adams,' one of them says. 'I hope we haven't disturbed you, but we'd like to talk to your daughter, Mrs Pearson, if that's all right.'

'Of course,' Mum says nervously. 'We'll leave you to it.'

'No, we can't interview her without one of you present, because she's a minor. That's the law.'

'Oh,' Mum says and sits down on the sofa.

'What's this all about?' Dad asks.

'We're just making further inquiries about the body found recently in the car fire nearby, and we think your daughter may have some information.'

134

'Right. Look, please sit down,' Dad says. The two detectives look around the room and sit together on the other sofa. Dad sits next to Mum. I'm the only one left standing. I take the armchair quickly.

'It's not usual we come and talk to people at this time of night,' Detective Shaw says. 'It's just that we read about Viola in the newspaper, and because of her disease we thought the evening would be the best time to come.'

'It's not a disease,' Mum says quickly. 'It's a condition, a rare genetic condition.'

'Just how do you think our daughter can help you?' Dad asks.

'Viola,' the one who called himself Detective Adams turns to me. He's trying not to stare, I can tell.

'I want to see your badges first,' I interrupt. It's what they do in the movies, always show their badges when they talk to someone. These two haven't done it.

'Viola, they said they were detectives. What else would they be?' Mum says.

'No, it's okay. We have identity cards in New Zealand, not badges,' Detective Shaw says. 'Here they are.' He takes a wallet out of his pocket, and so does the other one. They both slide plastic cards out of them, and Detective Shaw shows them to me. I glance at them, not knowing what I'm looking at, what I should be looking for. There's a photo of each of them, the words New Zealand Police. I hand them back.

'Shouldn't you be wearing stab-proof vests?' I ask.

They look at each other. Detective Shaw speaks again.

'We left them in the car, they're uncomfortable to wear and we didn't think we'd need them here tonight. You seem to know a lot.'

No one says anything to that. I'm waiting for him to continue – *You know a lot for a little kid. You know a lot for a kid that can only go out at night. You know a lot for a kid who's going to die.*

'Would you like a cup of tea, coffee?' Mum asks them.

'No, it's late, we won't keep you,' Detective Shaw says. 'It's just, well, we read the story in the newspaper about Viola and we're wondering if she was out in the forest the night of the car fire that occurred in this area on August twenty-fifth.'

'Yes, yes she was out that night,' Mum answers. 'I asked her about it, after the other police came the following day. She was asleep then, when they came. I didn't want to wake her.'

'Would she have been wearing the night-vision goggles that night?'

'Yes, of course. She always does. Otherwise she wouldn't be able to see anything.'

'Can we take a look at them?'

Mum glances at Dad, neither of them acknowledge me, then Dad gets up and leaves the room. I can hear him walking down the hallway to the laundry. He comes back carrying the goggles in their case. He's not sure which cop to hand them to until Detective Adams reaches out his hand.

'We bought them for her a few years ago. From the States,' Dad says, as he sits down again next to Mum.

Detective Adams is carefully taking the goggles out of the case, turning them over. 'They must be heavy to wear,' he says, looking at me.

I nod.

'Can you see well in them? Is it like daylight?'

I nod again, even though I haven't seen daylight for years.

'So that night, August twenty-fifth, did you see anything?' the other cop asks me.

I open my mouth. I'm going to tell him about the fat man and the money and Geoff Harris and about Jim and my morepork. I want to tell him; I want him to stop Geoff Harris.

'She told me she didn't see anything; I told you that,' Mum says.

'We wanted to ask Viola.'

'I didn't see anything.' I hear myself mumble my mother's words.

'There was a car fire. It should have lit up the night. With these you would have seen it from miles away.'

'I didn't see anything.'

'How many times do we have to tell you people?' Dad says, suddenly angry. 'Our daughter doesn't know anything. We would have rung you if we had any information.'

'The fire was unusually hot, for a car fire, and must have lasted for a long time,' Detective Adams says, putting the goggles and their case on the coffee table. 'Bodies don't burn easily and there was little left of the body when we found the car. The person who did it must have had another vehicle or left on foot. He may have left something behind. Maybe something your daughter has since found.'

'Have you found anything, anything at all, Viola?' Mum asks me, her eyes pleading.

I shake my head, not trusting my voice again.

'Well then, that's it,' Dad says getting up

The cops know they've been told to leave. They shuffle out of the room, following Dad. Mum packs the night-vision goggles away in their case.

Seventeen

The lights in McDonalds are dimmed. I'm not sure if this is because they have turned off all of the fluorescent lights, or they just think this is the way I like it. Do they want me to put on my night-vision goggles to read the menu above the counter or something? Anyway, I already know what I want. I looked at their range of burgers on the internet before we came. I want a Big Mac and fries and a Coke combo.

Mum orders a coffee.

We don't say anything while we find a table to eat at. There are a few other people sitting at tables, mostly lounging, but there is a guy and a girl who seem to be doing more kissing than eating. Mum concentrates on her coffee, which means I can stare at the couple kissing. Not so they notice me watching or anything like that;

I just take furtive glances between nibbling on fries and sipping the Coke.

I've never seen people kiss, not in real life. I mean, it's in the movies lots, but Mum and Dad don't do it. Not when I'm around anyway. I'm not sure what I think about it, or if I will ever get to do it one day with a guy. I don't even get to meet guys my own age, so the chances are pretty remote.

There was someone, I suppose, last year. But it wasn't a romance or anything. We just emailed a lot. He had XP too. He seemed to understand me and I understood him, but we were never going to meet. He was sixteen and he lived in Ohio.

And, anyway, he died.

His mum rang my mum with the news. Mum hadn't even known I was emailing a boy. She was pretty upset when she told me. His mum hadn't known either. Apparently, just before he died, he had asked his mum to ring me, to tell me so I wouldn't be waiting and wondering why he wasn't replying to my emails.

He hadn't told me he had cancer, that there was nothing the doctors could do, that they had gone through all the options and they had all failed. Keeping secrets, maybe it's what XP kids do, it's in our genetic makeup, an extra gene in place of the missing one on our DNA strands.

I stop watching the guy and the girl kiss and concentrate on eating the burger, which is really good. I like the pickles. Dad didn't come with us tonight, although he said he would have liked to. He has to get his sleep. We won't be back until one or two in the morning, so I didn't expect him to come and watch everyone look at the freak show. I'm not really sure if anyone in the restaurant knows who I am or why I'm here, which is good. No one at the counter said 'oh, you're that girl' or 'wow, you look awful'. Maybe the staff just got told to turn the lights down on this particular night and not why. After the art gallery and the museum it's a relief. I got like a royal escort around both. And the museum wasn't a normal museum, it was a car museum. Vintage, post-vintage, post-war and post-1960 cars, quoting from the brochure, and it was dead boring. The art gallery was interesting. They had a travelling exhibition of Hoteres there. The works were dark with lots of writing on them and lines intersecting.

Next week I get to go swimming. Yay.

Before we left the farm tonight, before Mum was ready, I slipped outside and checked my message to Geoff Harris. The car with the paper flames was gone, no longer tied to the tree where I left it. Only the string was still hanging from the branch. Geoff Harris has taken it. He now knows that I watched him burn the fat man in the car before following him to where he buried the money. He now knows he has to leave me and my parents alone.

Mum puts her coffee cup down and starts giggling.

'I'm so sorry,' she says.

'What about?'

'I mean, I took you to a car museum. A car museum.' She laughs again.

'So what's so funny?'

'A car museum. It was so boring and you, you were so interested. That old guy showing us around, he was so blown away that you liked his cars.'

'I didn't like his cars.'

'I know that, but you acted like you did. I'm so sorry. I thought it was going to be a real museum, not like that.'

'He was so into his cars.' I start to giggle now.

'I know; it was so funny. Watching the two of you. I'm so sorry. I'll check where they want to take us next time. No more car museums.'

'That would be good. I liked the Hoteres though.'

'I liked them too.'

The next night we start on the Vaughan Williams piece – *Prelude No. 1 from Suite for Viola and Orchestra*. It's okay. I can see Vaughan Williams's skill as a composer, how far music has come since Marais. Mum says some people think classical music is all Brahms and Beethoven, people long dead, but she thinks it's today's composers that are the exciting ones. She said they have something to say about the time we live in, and that it's important, that we continue to express ourselves. That's what Vaughan Williams was all about.

When we stop for the night she offers to make us both a hot chocolate. I follow her into the kitchen.

'Can you get the milk out of the fridge for me?' she asks.

As I close the fridge door I see a business card stuck behind a fridge magnet. It wasn't there last night. I see the name on it: 'Sam Baker, investment advisor.' It's the name from the car registration web site. It's the name of the person who owns the car Geoff Harris drove away in after burying the money. I feel as cold as the plastic container of milk I'm holding and it slips out of my hand and hits the floor.

'Viola, be careful.'

The container hasn't broken. I pick it up and take it to Mum who's frowning at me. She pours the milk into the two cups and hands it back. I put it in the fridge and look at the white business card again.

'Where did you get this?' I ask her, trying to sound casual, knowing that I'm not.

'What? Oh that man's card. He came around today.

Knocked on the door while we were both having lunch. He left us his card.'

'What does an investment advisor do?'

'Advises you what investments you should spend your money on.'

'What did he look like?'

'Why do you want to know?'

'Just want to know what an investment advisor looks like.'

'He had short blond hair, kind of thin, nice looking.'

'Did you let him in? Did he come inside?'

'Of course we did. We gave him some lunch. He had some interesting ideas. You know, the share market, that sort of thing. Oh, he asked after you. Said he had seen your story in the paper.'

'But you haven't got any money, have you, to invest?'

'Why do you think we would have money to invest?'

'You haven't, have you?'

'No.'

'And you told him that?'

'Well, he had spent so much trouble coming all the way out here that we said we'd think about it and get back to him.'

'But he doesn't think you have any money?'

'I don't know what he thinks. Why all the questions?'

'Nothing. Just weird there are people out there looking for people with money.'

It's a lame answer but Mum seems to accept it. I look again at the card. There is an Ashburton post-office box number and a mobile phone number on it. No street address, nothing to show where he actually is. The mail from the post-office box could be forwarded to anywhere. Or he could get someone else to pick it up.

Later, after Mum has gone to bed, I check the money in the envelope is still behind the clock on the mantelpiece. It is. I sit at the dining table, where Geoff Harris, dope grower and murderer, now pretending to be Sam Baker, investment advisor, would have sat having lunch with my parents while I slept upstairs. He wouldn't have been able to see the envelope from the table. But what if they had let him wander around the living room? Would he have seen it then?

I put on the night-vision goggles and slip outside into the night, run over to where I had left the toy car, my message to Geoff Harris, Sam Baker, whatever his name is now, to stay away. I search through the pine needles and there it is. The rain from the other night must have destroyed the sellotape so the car fell out of the string noose. The tiny paper flames are mush, buried by the wind.

He didn't get my message at all.

Inside, I take the business card from under the fridge magnet and throw it into the fireplace. I watch it burn.

Eighteen

My correspondence teacher has rung Mum. Apparently I'm falling behind in my school work. She's worried about me. Wondering if there is anything happening at home that she should know about.

I eat the eggs at the table listening to Mum ask me, for the thousandth time, what is wrong.

'You're still locking the doors at night, aren't you?'

I chew the toast slowly.

'What is up with you? Is it because of Jim dying? Are you upset about that? We could get you a puppy. Is that what you want?'

'No.' I almost shout the word.

Mum stands, her back against the kitchen bench, tea towel in her hands, and stares at me.

'Really, I'm okay. I'll get onto my school work. I'm

sorry. I've just been spending too much time in the forest.'

'You haven't even being doing that. Most nights you hardly go out.'

'Look, I'm sorry. I'll get my school work done.'

I run up the stairs to my bedroom. The eggs were mostly finished anyway. I jump onto my bed, open my laptop and start going through my emails and my lessons and what I should have been doing. Tomorrow night is the big swimming night at the Ashburton pool so I'd better get some schoolwork done now. I pick the maths to start on. Logic, as I well know, doesn't have emotions, and I soon lose myself in graphs and equations that plot lines between the x axis and the y axis. I can do the work without thinking about anything else, treat it as a puzzle, a game, let it take my full attention so I don't worry about the cancer in my body and Geoff Harris and the police and the nice people of Ashburton who want me to use their swimming pool.

I try not to think about Mum's offer of a puppy.

The next night she's silent on the drive into Ashburton. I wonder if she's decided whether to take the fulltime job with the orchestra, maybe that's what she's thinking about. It would mean she would only be home at weekends, and only when they weren't performing on a Saturday night or on tour out of the country. I want her to take it. We can cope without her, Dad and I, and it's what she's good at. It's what she should do. And she would be safer in Wellington. When Geoff Harris comes to kill us all there will only be me and Dad then.

No one said anything about the missing business card from the fridge door. Maybe they were never going to ring Samuel Baker anyway. Even so, I haven't put any more money in envelopes in the mailbox, just in case. I wonder how much he found out about us, while he sat and ate lunch. Does he now know that the guns are kept in the woolshed, that Dad usually goes to bed early, that their daughter can shoot a rabbit at least a paddock away?

I have put a big, flesh-coloured plaster on the sore on my wrist.

A woman meets us at the swimming pool. She's not that old, younger than my mum anyway. She says her name is Pip.

'I understand you don't know how to swim,' she says to me.

I nod looking back at Mum who gives me one of her encouraging smiles.

'Well, I'll be with you the whole time and, if you want to, I can teach you a few things. Let's get you into your bathing suit first.'

She shows me where the changing room is. There's a

private cubicle so I use that. There are a few women in the main changing room. They kind of look at me, I try to ignore them.

The bathing suit still feels strange against my skin. I cover myself up with my towel when I walk back towards the pool and Pip. She and Mum have been talking, obviously, as they both stop suddenly when they see me. Mum takes my bag with my clothes in it.

'Have fun,' she says simply.

Pip leads me round to where there are stairs going into the water. A few people are in the pool, mostly swimming up and down the length, ropes dividing them from each other, I suppose, so they don't collide.

'We're usually closing by this time, but we've kept the complex open for you,' Pip says as she lowers herself into the water. 'All the fluorescent lights have been turned off as well, so you don't have to worry about anything.'

Don't have to worry about anything. Yeah, right. At least she isn't staring at me.

'Just come into the water. It's not deep, look it's only up to my waist and it's not cold.'

I start into the water. It might not be cold but it's not hot, and her waist equals about my chest. I kind of bob around a bit, hopping from one foot to the other, not sure what to do, not sure if I like this one little bit.

I feel so naked, so exposed. I'm only ever like this in the shower at home, when the door is firmly shut. Usually, even in my bedroom, I have two or three layers of clothes on.

'Just walk around in the water, get used to it, and then we'll put our heads under.'

Our heads under? You have got to be kidding.

'It will be fine,' she says. She must have seen the look on my face.

After half an hour, Pip not only has me blowing bubbles with my eyes open under the water, she also has me floating like a starfish and using what she calls a board and kicking part way along the length of the pool. It's kind of fun.

I shower and get dried and dressed again, then find Mum and Pip talking by the side of the pool. This time I catch what they are saying.

'If you want to, if she wants to, we could have a swimming lesson once a week. It wouldn't be a problem.'

'But it's getting lighter and lighter with summer,' Mum is trying to explain. 'You'd have to keep the pool open to midnight. We have to drive here first and we can't do that until it's dark.'

'Well, in the winter then. That wouldn't be a problem for us and it's only six months away.'

'Would you like that?' Mum asks me.

'Yes, in the winter.' It's easy to agree to things I don't think I will be around for.

Neither of us says much on the trip home towards the mountains. I'm still excited about swimming, even though I'll probably never get the chance to do it again. The winter is a long time away. But I can add it to my practical list of things to do before I die and then I can cross it off. My floundering around could vaguely be called swimming. Anyway, I'm the judge, so swimming is crossed off.

Mum makes me a hot chocolate when we get home. Dad has already gone to bed.

'So, are you going to tell me what's wrong with your wrist?' she asks as she hands me the cup.

I quickly look down at my arm, but my sleeve is covering the bandage. She must have seen it when I was in the pool.

'Actually, don't even tell me. Show me.'

I put the cup down on the table and let her pull the sleeve up, take off the plaster. She hauls me under the light to take a closer look.

'It's only been like that for a week, really. I don't think it's anything.'

'I'll call your doctor in the morning. I'll make an appointment.'

'If it's cancer, Mum, I don't want to do all the stuff.'

'If it's cancer we'll figure out what we're going to do when we find out it's cancer. Is this what you've been worrying about? Oh, Viola. You should have just told me.'

'I don't want to have chemo.'

'I don't know if you have to have chemo. If you have to have it then that's when we'll talk about. I don't want you upset about something that may never happen. Look, I'll get an appointment as soon as possible but please don't worry about it until then.'

'Okay.'

'Now go do some more school work for that dragon of a teacher of yours.'

'Mum?'

'Yes?'

'The job at the symphony orchestra, I think you should take it.'

'Why do you say that?'

'I just think you should.'

'But then I wouldn't be able to look after you. I wouldn't be home like I am now.'

'I'd be all right. You don't have to worry about me.'

She looks at me, startled.

'I'll go do some schoolwork.'

Nineteen

Mum must have been really worried about me, either my state of mind or whatever it is on my wrist, because the next night we're driving back through the Canterbury plains, past all the dairy farms again and into Ashburton. My doctor, Dr Marshall, although I'm meant to call him Don, works at the hospital. Every six months I have an appointment with him and I know he looks forward to seeing me as much as I dread it. Of course, I'm his only XP patient and, even better, for him anyway, he is the only doctor in New Zealand who has an XP patient, which makes him special, he says. He's the one who explained to me about genetics and Mendel's squares, and I admit it, he is okay, if just a little bit over enthusiastic.

It's still two months to go to my normal appointment

but he's happy to see me so soon. 'It's not a problem at all, anytime,' he tells Mum. He and I discuss vampires as small talk to begin with, then he asks to see my wrist. He takes a long look at the sore then moves my arm around under a light. Then he gets these glasses out that look like tiny binoculars and puts them on and has another look. Mum fidgets next to me.

'You know, I don't think you have anything to worry about here,' Dr Marshall, Don, says.

'What is it?' Mum asks.

'It's certainly not a melanoma. It's not skin cancer.'

'But what is it then?'

'Viola, have you been taking your vitamin D pills?'

'Yes. At breakfast.'

'She has breakfast at night, when she gets up,' Mum explains.

'How many are you taking?' Don asks.

'Just one.'

'Well then, I think that's the problem. You should be taking at least three. One a day is for healthy people who are still getting some sunlight. You get none at all.'

'But you've always told me to take just one.'

'That was when you were little. Take three now, starting from when you get home tonight. Look after those bones.'

'That's what has caused the sore, not enough vitamin D?' Mum asks, not believing in such a simple answer. No doubt she had been ready to fight me so I would have surgery and chemotherapy and anything else it took to keep me alive for a few more years.

'I think so. I'll give you some cream that will help it heal up. Now let's have a look at the rest of you.'

I sigh as it means taking off all my clothes except my undies and him staring closely at my skin. He's been doing it since I was a baby but I still feel uncomfortable.

'Well, we might as well, since you're here. Then you can go away and not worry about anything,' he says with a smile.

He has a diagram of my body with every mole, every freckle I have, mapped on it. He uses it to check for anything new, or anything that has changed.

'She's fine,' he says to Mum afterwards. 'She's doing a good job, looking after herself, staying out of the sun.'

I'm dressed now, relieved it is all over.

'I read that article about you in the paper,' he says. 'It was great, except you could have talked about me in it.' He's laughing; he doesn't care. He's just giving me a hard time.

I apologise. I didn't think of it. The reporter didn't ask.

He has a few more lame vampire jokes for me (I

heard being a vampire really sucks. Where do vampires have their savings accounts? In a blood bank) then we all say goodbye. I don't have to see him for another six months, which will make it after Christmas, so he wishes me Merry Christmas and Happy New Year and asks if I'll be waiting up for Santa Claus. Maybe with my night-vision goggles I might be able to spot him and his reindeer landing on our farm-house roof. I'm about to tell him I figured out Santa Claus isn't real a few years ago, that I'm not a kid anymore, but hey, we've just been discussing vampires for the last half hour so I give up.

On the drive home, Mum starts talking again about the concert they want me to play in. The Mid-Canterbury Young People's Orchestra is having an end-of-year performance at the Ashburton Events Centre and they want me to perform a piece, just one piece, which I can choose. It will be a solo, I will be standing in front of the orchestra, a spotlight on me.

'Why can't I just play as part of the orchestra, like you do?'

'Viola, this orchestra has been playing all year together. Most of them are school kids. They don't have time to have a new viola player coming in at the last minute. Maybe next year we could look at doing something like that.'

'I don't want a spotlight. I don't want any lights on me.'

'A spotlight won't damage your skin; it's not a fluorescent light.'

'I don't want one.'

'But how will you see your music?'

'I'll learn it off by heart.'

'But how will the orchestra see, the conductor? You can't play on a pitch black stage.'

'Okay, some light, no spotlight.'

'No spotlight. Agreed. Right. What do you want to play?'

'*Meditation*.'

'That's a good choice. People will enjoy that and you play it really nicely.'

The conversation over, I stare out of the car window. There are stars out, only the mountains before us blocking them with their darkness. I press my cheek against the cold glass of the window and think about the possums in the forest, wonder what they will be up to. I wonder what secrets the trees will be whispering, whether they miss me, whether they even realise I haven't been visiting lately. If I took the twenty-two into the forest, even with the night-vision goggles, I still wouldn't be safe. Geoff Harris could be waiting for me; he could take the gun off me, use it against me.

He's bigger than I am. Stronger. And anyway, he has a shotgun. Shotguns kill people easier than twenty-twos. You don't have to be so accurate; the pellets spread wide; they're more deadly than a single, small bullet. A twenty-two has greater range but you have to be a good shot, be able to stay calm and cool and stand steady to shoot well. You can't kill someone if you're running through a forest with a twenty-two. You could with a shotgun, if you were close enough. I could take my dad's shotgun with me, but last time I fired it my shoulder hurt for days and, even wearing earmuffs, my ears were ringing. It's too heavy. I can't run with it.

I could just tell everyone. Tell Mum and Dad and the detectives who came and visited about the fat man and the car fire and the money and how Geoff Harris has a new identity as Sam Baker, that he's not dead at all, that they're looking for the wrong person, and then the detectives can go arrest Geoff Harris and it will all be over.

But maybe the detectives will find him by themselves. Maybe this will finish in a few more days and then I don't have to tell anyone and I can keep the money and give it to Mum and Dad like I have been and save the farm.

I just have to wait a few more days, a few more weeks.

Twenty

Mum has to go to Wellington again. She won't be long. Only for two nights. She's going to take my viola with her, get new strings for it, the pegs reshaped. Its sound has become dull, lost its vibrancy, she says. She can't wait for me to hear what it will sound like restrung.

I can tell she's still worried about me, the way she looks at me, the concern in her voice even when she's talking about really boring stuff like my vitamin pills and my school work (which is now all up to date). I'm still locking all the doors at night, still watching at windows from darkened rooms, forehead against the glass, looking out. Maybe that's what it is. The sore on my wrist is better, either thanks to me swallowing a fistful of vitamin D each day or the cream my doctor gave me. I feel better; I feel more in control. I don't have cancer. I'm not going to die. I'm going to play the viola in front of an audience. Maybe Mum will let me do a music exam next year, in the winter, when the sun sets early, and I will learn how to swim. Suddenly, next year is full of possibilities. This year is slowly dying, almost over, the shortest night not far off and then I can start to reclaim the twilights and the forest. By that time Geoff Harris will be caught or gone. Maybe it has already happened.

There has been no sign of him, so I have started going back into the forest but not venturing far, not back to where the money was buried, or where the car fire was. Just far enough so I can feel the cool breeze on my face and listen to the trees and watch for any of the night animals or birds. In summer, our house changes from a fridge into an oven. The blackout curtains on my bedroom windows stop the light but not the heat during the day and I don't sleep well. If I open the windows to let in the air the wind can blow the curtains so much that sunlight seeps in. Anyway, in a Canterbury summer the air outside is just as hot as inside. It's a baking heat which turns the farm brown and the pine needles yellow. Dad gets nervous about feed and starts to wean and draft the early lambs to send away. If they are heavy enough they will go to the works. Otherwise they are sold to other farmers, who will have a go at fattening them. If things get really bad, Dad starts feeding out the hay he holds back from the winter every year. This is the time he should be making hay, but sometimes he has to feed it out instead. One rain is all it takes to make the difference, to make the grass green up and grow again, to make everything all right. That's what he's waiting for now. Rain.

He won't be able to take me out on the farm when Mum is in Wellington. He'll be asleep before it is dusk, the evenings are so drawn out. I won't even see him. We will pass each other's doors while each is sleeping. It will be like living on my own. But it will only be for a few days, Mum says. I'll be fine.

I put another ten thousand in an envelope in the mailbox two nights before she goes so she can bank it with the others while she's there. The next day the opened envelope is behind the mantelpiece clock. Maybe I could just jam all the money in there. It would save me having to walk out to the mailbox each time.

The first night she's gone I wake up hot in my stuffy room. The house is quiet. Dad must already be in bed. I find my jeans and a T-shirt and get dressed. It's no cooler downstairs. There's left-over cooked chicken in the fridge, and I make myself a sandwich with lettuce and lots of mayonnaise. Pour myself a glass of milk, take my vitamin D capsules, glance through the newspaper left on the table. The forecast is for sunshine, at least for the next five days.

I turn out all the lights in the house, go to the back door and take my night-vision goggles from their case. Outside, it is so warm I don't even need a sweatshirt. Mum has my viola so I can't play in the woolshed. I head towards the trees instead.

The forest welcomes me with a tired sigh. Even though its roots are deep into Canterbury's aquifers, the pine needles are dry and dusty. They want a shower of rain to tidy themselves up, to feel fresh again. I wander a few rows in and sit against a tree trunk and look around, see what there is to see. The forest looks empty. The white trees vertical against the background of darkness and night-vision green.

Next to me, between two low branches, a fat spider is spinning a web. I watch, as still as I can. It doesn't seem to notice. It has already spun the cross lines and is now working from the centre, circling slowly as it spins its glistening trap.

'Get up, slowly. Don't try anything.' Something cold and hard sticks into my shoulder. It's a gun.

I do as the voice says. It's Geoff Harris. I don't have to turn around to figure it out. It's the same voice that called into the darkness months ago when he gave up digging the holes, looking for his money; it's the same smell of sweat.

'Take off the night-vision glasses.'

I turn my head around for a second, seeing if he'll let me refuse, but he jabs the gun again into my back. I fumble with the straps.

'Put them on the ground.'

I do as he says, even though his voice is trembling. He seems scared, hyped up, nervous. 'Now move away from them.'

I take a few steps to my right, blinded by the darkness. I can hardly see the tree next to me. If it is this dark I could make a run for it, he wouldn't be able to see me to follow. Then he switches on a torch.

'Start walking. That way.' He shines the beam in front of me. He wants me to walk away from the house, into the forestry. Dad, if he is awake, will never hear me scream out for help unless I do it now, but my throat is dry. I couldn't make a sound if I wanted to. Geoff Harris pokes me again with the long gun barrel, pushing me forward, the way he wants me to go. He already has my night-vision goggles over his arm. I stumble forward. The torch beam is all over the place, and I walk into a tree.

He laughs, crazily. 'Now you know what it feels

like. All that time I was running through this forest, you were following me, weren't you? I was crashing into trees and you were just watching, weren't you? Weren't you?'

'Yes,' I rasp.

'Now you know what it feels like.'

'Where are we going?'

'Doesn't matter.'

I start walking again, my hands out in front of me to feel for tree trunks, low branches. I'm not used to being in the dark. Not in the forest. I stumble over roots, stones, through deep drifts of pine needles. The torch beam jumps past me. Geoff Harris is right behind.

The forest has gone quiet. Still. It's listening, watching, seeing who will win this battle. Slowly I begin to see, the dark shapes as I move closer to them become clearer, the dark not dark at all, but a myriad of shades of grey. I realise where I am and change course slightly. He doesn't notice. Maybe he has no clear idea of where he's taking me, as long as it's away from the house. I continue to drift to the right, taking him deeper into the forest, towards the slope with its slippery pine needles and the steep drop into the river.

We walk for at least an hour, maybe longer. In the dark I can't see my watch. All I know is that now I can hear the river chattering over the stones and that's an hour's walk from the house, a normal walk, with me wearing my night-vision goggles.

Just as the forest floor starts to slope downwards, to the drop off over the river, he tells me to sit down. I slump next to the nearest tree, my back to the trunk, as close to it as I can be, my knees drawn up to my chin. There is still time. *Don't panic*, I tell myself. *There is still time*.

He walks around and crouches a couple of metres away, plays the torch beam on my face then puts it on the ground so he can see me and I can see him. He has the shotgun pointed at me.

'Tell me where you have my money.' The walk through the dark has worn him out, frayed his nerves even more. 'If you don't tell me, I will shoot you. I shot that morepork. You found it didn't you?'

'You killed Jim too.'

'Jim? Who's Jim?'

'My dog. You killed my dog.'

'I didn't kill any damn dog I just killed your morepork. The one you talked about in the newspaper. That night I shot it, there was thunder and lightning. You wouldn't have heard it, wouldn't have heard the gun go off. No one will hear it go off now either. We're in the middle of nowhere. There's no one around. No one to save you.'

I don't say anything, keep my head down, listen to the river chattering.

'Where's my money?'

'I don't have your money.' My voice sounds croaky, scared.

'I'll shoot you.'

'If you shoot me then I won't be able to tell you, will I?'

My logic shuts him up.

'I don't have your money,' I try again. Maybe he'll let me go, if I make him believe me. Maybe he doesn't have to end up in the river.

'Oh, you do. Of course you do. You haven't spent it. I've never seen you wearing any pretty dresses. But your parents could do with the money. You know I talked to them? Had lunch with them. They need the money. Your mum is away, isn't she?'

'How do you know?'

'It was on the orchestra's website. I've been watching it. It said in that newspaper article that your mum played in the orchestra. I've been patient. Waiting for her to leave you. I know from talking to them over lunch, you were sleeping upstairs, that your dad doesn't check up on you, not like your mum does. He'll get up tomorrow morning and won't even realise you're not in your room. I don't even have to shoot you. If you don't tell me where my money is then we'll just wait until the sun comes up and that will kill you. Won't it? Not straight away. It will be slower than that. More painful. A child so young dying of cancer. You've never felt the sun on your face have you?'

'No,' I whisper, as a tear rolls down my cheek.

Twenty-one

'You've never gone swimming at the beach, never been sunbathing, never played sport outside, never done anything, have you, Viola?' Geoff Harris says, sitting down, slowly stretching his legs out in front of him.

I'm still frozen against the tree trunk, the forest still and silent around me. There is just him and me and my night-vision goggles lying on the pine needles between us, the torch and its beam, the shotgun in his hands pointed at me. From somewhere close I can hear a wild piglet calling for its mother.

'That's what the story in the paper said, so I'll be giving you a new experience. We've only got about another four hours before dawn, and it takes an hour at least to walk back to your home, so I think you should start talking or you are going to feel that sun for the very first time.'

I hug my legs closer to my chest. I'm cold. My bare arms now shaking, covered in goose bumps.

'I can see this is going to take a while for you to figure it all out, but I can wait. I can be patient.'

We sit. He stares at me. I look down at my feet in the torch light, at the pine needles.

He picks up my night-vision goggles with one hand, the other still holds the shotgun on me.

'How do these work anyway?' He takes a quick look through them. 'Can't see a thing.'

'You have to focus them to your eyesight.'

'Really? Don't need them anyway. I have my torch and soon it will be daylight. Forecast is for a glorious morning, you know. Not a cloud in the sky. Going to be a hot one. So where's my money? You watched me bury it that night didn't you?'

'No.'

'Liar. You must have seen me haul James into my car and set it alight. Then you followed me through the trees. What happened? You came back later that night with a spade of your own? Dug another hole and buried it there?'

'No.'

'Liar, liar, your pants will catch on fire.' He suddenly

laughs, the noise cutting through the trees. 'That's going to be kind of true, isn't it? When the sun comes up you are going to burn, just like my mate James. As soon as it starts getting hot you are going to be begging me for help. You'll tell me everything then. You'll lead me to the spot where you buried my money and all this will be done with.'

I don't say anything.

'I mean, what good is a million dollars to someone like you? You can't spend it.'

He yawns, and I hear him settling back against a tree trunk. 'You're keeping me up past my bedtime, you know,' he says, yawning again.

My head keeps on telling me to run, to take my chances, to lead him to the drop off to the river, but my body has gone cold and stiff from sitting for so long. Would I be able to run fast enough, weave from side to side to dodge the shotgun pellets, stop myself slipping over the edge too?

And he's not going to fall asleep, not asleep enough that I can creep away without waking him. I can't even see his face properly to tell if he's asleep, to tell if I should risk it. The light of the torch is on me, not him.

I think about Dad safe in the house, about Mum in Wellington, about the sun coming up. The forest is waiting, wondering what I'm going to do. All I can hear is the river down the slope, rushing through its narrow channels, past its rocks and its boulders. I can't tell Geoff Harris where his money is, because that will take him to the woolshed, take him back towards the house. Dad will hear the noise, wake up, confront the stranger who is holding a gun to his daughter's head, and he will be shot. Geoff Harris will kill him. It's better that I die, not Dad. I'm going to die one day anyway. And I haven't got all the money to give back to him. Some of it Mum and Dad have. I hug my legs tighter, trying to get warm, my cheek on my knees, my tears making my jeans wet. Mum always says the coldest hours are the ones just before dawn.

I wait for the sun.

I don't know how much time passes. Every now and then Geoff Harris mumbles something, shifts his hands on the gun, tries to get more comfortable on the pine needles. I think about how much sunlight will reach the forest floor, whether it will be enough. I don't know. I've never been out under the trees in the day. If it isn't, if the dawn comes and the sun doesn't reach the pine needles will he march me out onto the forestry road? Will he risk a car driving past, or a forestry truck, risk being seen with a shotgun and a girl standing for the first time in the sun?

The piglet I heard earlier squeals again. It's closer than before. Another squeal. There must be more than one. Then I hear the mother, the sow. It's snuffling in the pine needles over to my left. The sound makes the hairs on the back of my neck shoot straight up.

Geoff Harris grabs the torch and starts waving it towards the noise.

'What was that?'

I don't answer. I think of all the things my dad has told me about wild pigs, about how a sow with piglets is more dangerous than even a boar, how a boar will probably run away, if you yell at it, but a sow will stay and protect its young, it will charge at you, chase you, and you must never run. Never ever run. It will always run faster than you. Instead, walk away slowly; give it space; let it go back to its young.

The sow grunts again. I can hear it moving through the pine needles.

'What is that?' Geoff Harris yells at me. He mustn't have heard a wild pig before. I remember him running through the forest with the bag of money, how he had not brought a torch then, how the possums had scared him. Geoff Harris is a city person. He doesn't know the forest.

'What is that?' he yells at me again.

I almost tell him to stop yelling and turn off the

torch, to stay still and quiet and just let the wild pig leave with her piglets.

But I don't.

His torch beam finally catches the sow. In the light I can see its small black eyes, its nose covered in dirt and pine needles. If I didn't know what it was, I would have thought it was some sort of monster, something out of a nightmare. The sow looks straight into the torch beam and then runs towards it, towards Geoff Harris holding onto the torch. The wild pig is huge. I'm on my feet, backing away. Geoff Harris is fumbling with the shot gun, trying to hold the torch and fire the gun at the same time. He gets one shot off, but it's too high, maybe one or two pellets hit the pig, but it's not enough to stop it. The noise echoes around the trees, deafening me. I pull closer to the tree. Geoff Harris takes off running, the sow right at his feet. He weaves through the trees, the torch light bobbing as he runs. Then there is a scream. A long scream that suddenly stops. The torch light is gone.

I wait. I hear the sow come back, snuffling and grunting as before, finding its piglets. I listen to its breath as it moves past, scuffing the pine needles with its feet. It ignores me. Maybe it knows me, recognises me as one of the smells that should be here, that is part of the forest.

The sow and the piglets move off together, into the trees. It's quiet again. I wait but still there's nothing. Only the stars through the gaps in the trees give me any light, and that is not enough to see even the trunks of the trees around me. I bend down unsteadily, patting around the forest floor through the pine needles, searching for my night-vision goggles. At last my fingers find the hard plastic straps.

It takes a while for me to refocus them. Geoff Harris altered all the settings when he tried to use them. Without a light, something for my eyes to focus on, it is hard, almost impossible but I manage it using the tops of the trees in the starlight. I start off, carefully, after him. His trail is simple to find.

The sow chased him towards the river. Even before I edge my way down the slope, I know what has happened. Where he started to slide in the pine needles is easy to see. I get down on all fours and crawl slowly to the edge, hang onto the last pine tree and look down into the deep gorge.

His body is under the water. There is blood on the boulder next to the pool. He never had a chance.

Twenty-two

Dawn is already glimmering over the water, making the foam whiter in the night-vision goggles. I have to get home. I carefully crawl back up the slope and then run through the forest like I have never run before. The trees are quiet around me, watching, waiting to see if I will make it before the sun comes up. They seem to make their rows neat and tidy for me, leading me home, so I don't have to weave through them. They pull in their roots so I won't trip over them. But I'm too late. Daylight is already reaching down, its fingers of light touching the pine needles. I'm not going to make it.

I stop, my chest heaving, my heart thumping, and pull off the heavy goggles, they are no use to me now. I try to see the darkest part of the forest. But none of it is dark, there is light everywhere.

The sun is up.

My jeans and my shoes and socks are enough to cover my legs but my T-shirt is thin, my head and arms bare. I need sunblock, sunglasses, a hat, a face cloth, a jacket. I've got none of these. I think about going back to the river for Geoff Harris' jacket but I don't know if I could make it down the bank, don't know how deep his body is under the water. And anyway, it's too late.

I look up at the trees. I plead to them to help me, to protect me until it is dark again, and then I look down at the pine needles and know what I have to do. With my hands I frantically push piles of them together until I have a huge heap and I bury myself in them. I can still breathe. The damp earth is cool against my skin, the smell of mustiness and dirt comforting. I'm safe.

Somehow I fall asleep.

I wake hours later, but the sun must still be shining; the pine needles above me are hot. I bury myself deeper, carefully checking that every last part of my skin is covered, and trying to ignore my dry throat, my rumbling stomach, my shirt sticking to my back with sweat.

I try to sleep again but I can't. I need to pee. My mind searches for something to think about to stop the panic that is quickly rising in my chest. At last it grasps onto the final few notes of *Meditation*. I force it to start at the beginning, to concentrate on each note, what it looks like in my music book, how it feels under my bow, how it sounds. Note after note, seperately, then together, bar after bar, page after page.

I play it three times through and when I open my eyes again it's dark.

At first I don't know where I am, why there is this weight on top of me. I dig myself out of the pine needles and fit the night-vision goggles on, start for home. I look out for the places I know, the signposts showing me the way back. When I get there, the house is dark. There are no police cars parked outside, no search being hurriedly organised for me. Dad mustn't have realised I was missing. And now he's gone to bed.

And I'm starving. And I so need a shower.

I creep into the house. The back door is unlocked. I turn on the lights, carefully pack the night-vision goggles away in their case. Everything looks the same, like it always does, like nothing has changed.

I find some bread in the pantry and stuff a couple of slices straight into my mouth, not even bothering with butter or jam or anything, not even bothering to wash my hands first. I go upstairs, step over the fifth stair, and pause at my parents' bedroom. The door is slightly ajar. Dad is snoring. It is the best sound I think I have ever heard.

I stop at my own doorway. Through the gap I can just make out my bed. The duvet is heaped in the middle. Even to me it looks as if I'm sleeping under it. I can't blame Dad for not realising I was gone all day. If he ever knew, if he and Mum ever knew anything about it, I can't imagine what would happen. They don't need to know. It will be my secret forever, and the sow's and her piglets. Maybe someone will find the body. Maybe no one will.

Maybe, in a few years from now, when it doesn't matter, when I am hooked up to machines keeping me alive as cancer finally takes my body, I will tell my parents then. Tell them where to find the last of the money, that I have run out of time to put in their mail box. Tell them once again to use it wisely.

After I shower and get dressed, put my clothes in the washing machine with the powder and start the cycle, I find a pie in the freezer and stick it in the microwave on high, turn on the grill in the oven ready. I watch the pie go around and around inside the microwave, and suddenly I have to sit down.

It's over, I suddenly realise. It's really over this time.

The next night, when I get up, Mum is waiting for me. She's back from Wellington. She gives me a weird look, as if there is something different about me but she doesn't know what. She tells me she has thought long and hard about the contract with the symphony orchestra and decided the time isn't right yet. The job will always be waiting for her, but for now she wants to be home with Dad and with me. She enjoys being out on the farm too much. She would miss the mountains. I give her a hug.

'That's not like you,' she says, surprised.

'What?'

'Hugging people.'

I shrug my shoulders. She turns back to my eggs cooking in the pot.

'I got the new strings for your viola,' she says. 'You should hear how it plays now.'

'Mum, I've been thinking, you know about this concert, at the events centre in Ashburton.'

'What about it?'

'Well, I think I would like to have the lights on when I play.'

'They wanted to have a spotlight on you. I've already told them no.'

'Can you ring them again?'

'Why?'

'It's just that, I think a spotlight will be okay.'